"What do we do now?" she asked.

"We stay here, safe and together, while my family watches for signs of his return and I keep you out of sight." Cruz turned his lips toward her head. "You should probably get some sleep," he said softly.

"I won't be able to sleep," she said. "And I don't want to be alone. Do you mind if I stay with you a little longer?"

His heart gave a heavy kick and he fumbled for how best to respond. Gina was soft and warm against him.

"All right." He adjusted her in his arms, so her head rested against his chest. Then he let himself relax and enjoy the moment, delighted that she wanted to be there with him, too, even if it was only to avoid being alone. And he wished, self-indulgently, that one day soon he could tell her exactly how little he minded her choosing him over an empty room and bed.

And how much he'd like her to choose him again every night.

STAY HIDDEN

JULIE ANNE LINDSEY

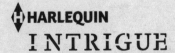

This one is for Catherine Fisher

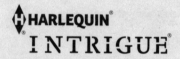

HARLEQUIN®
INTRIGUE®

Recycling programs
for this product may
not exist in your area.

ISBN-13: 978-1-335-55540-3

Stay Hidden

Copyright © 2021 by Julie Anne Lindsey

All rights reserved. No part of this book may be used or reproduced in
any manner whatsoever without written permission except in the case of
brief quotations embodied in critical articles and reviews.

This is a work of fiction. Names, characters, places and incidents
are either the product of the author's imagination or are used fictitiously.
Any resemblance to actual persons, living or dead, businesses,
companies, events or locales is entirely coincidental.

This edition published by arrangement with Harlequin Books S.A.

For questions and comments about the quality of this book,
please contact us at CustomerService@Harlequin.com.

Harlequin Enterprises ULC
22 Adelaide St. West, 40th Floor
Toronto, Ontario M5H 4E3, Canada
www.Harlequin.com

Printed in U.S.A.

Julie Anne Lindsey is an obsessive reader who was once torn between the love of her two favorite genres: toe-curling romance and chew-your-nails suspense. Now she gets to write both for Harlequin Intrigue. When she's not creating new worlds, Julie can be found carpooling her three kids around northeastern Ohio and plotting with her shamelessly enabling friends. Winner of the Daphne du Maurier Award for Excellence in Mystery/Suspense, Julie is a member of International Thriller Writers, Romance Writers of America and Sisters in Crime. Learn more about Julie and her books at julieannelindsey.com.

Visit the Author Profile page at Harlequin.com.

CAST OF CHARACTERS

Gina Ricci—Four months pregnant and on the run from her former abuser and ex-boyfriend, Tony Marino, Gina will stop at nothing to protect her baby from the child's father, who's becoming more dangerous by the day.

Cruz Winchester—A PI falling fast for the beautiful, strong and caring woman who stumbled into his life hoping to disappear. Now he'll do anything to keep her safe, find her stalker and maybe earn the right to be her permanent personal protection.

Derek Winchester—Cruz's partner at their PI firm, a cousin by blood and brother by upbringing. Always willing to help his family any way he can.

Knox Winchester—A Great Falls, Kentucky, deputy sheriff and the younger brother of Cruz Winchester, committed to helping protect Gina Ricci and put Tony Marino behind bars.

Blaze Winchester—West Liberty homicide detective, assisting his brothers and cousin in the protection of Gina Ricci and capture of Tony Marino.

Kayla Ricci—Gina's younger sister, a college student determined to help bring Gina home safely, however she can.

Tony Marino—Gina Ricci's ex-boyfriend and the father of her unborn child, intent on getting his hands on Gina by any means possible and punishing her for leaving him.

Chapter One

Gina Ricci hurried through the cool fall night, pushed by a mounting sense of dread at her core. Normally she enjoyed the short walk home following an evening shift at the animal shelter, but this time something wasn't right. She could feel it in her bones. On the air and in the rain.

She pressed a palm against her gently rounded middle, reminding herself that her deranged ex-boyfriend, Tony, couldn't reach her, or her unborn child, here. "It's okay," she whispered, steeling her nerves and comforting her baby. "I did everything right this time, and there's no way he's here." The words had become a mantra after moving to Great Falls, Kentucky, her fourth stop in two long months of hiding. She'd learned to deal in cash only, and rented an apartment with a building manager willing to forgo the background and credit check. Found work, solitude and a doctor who'd see her without health insurance.

This time, Gina had hope.

She flipped her hood up against the finely misting rain and hurried along the sidewalk toward her building. Around her, the small downtown streets had begun their nightly transition, as quaint shops closed and local honky-tonks opened.

Gina counted her paces, thinking of the cool sheen of water floating on the breeze instead of all the things that could go wrong. Her muscles were tense but fatigued from a long day of work at BFF Rescue, and she could use a nice relaxing shower. Six hours of helping animals and humans find their next best friend forever through photos often left her tired and sweaty, not to mention covered in hair. She loved grooming and outfitting prospective pet adoptees, then uploading their images to the rescue's website. There were no photos of sad animals behind bars on her watch. Gina made sure every picture was dating-app-worthy and showcased the dog's or cat's personality. She even added a nice bio for each animal that included their likes and dislikes. "Loves kids!" for some. "Cranky old lady in search of silence and servitude" for others. If she could, she'd take every pet home with her, but despite her new apartment, Gina was one step away from homeless too.

Her family would be horrified if they knew what she was going through, and she missed them so much it hurt. But it wasn't about her, or them, anymore. Not since the moment a doctor had told her she was pregnant, and she'd known instantly she'd guard the child with her life, to the very end. Especially from its father.

If Tony knew there was a human in the world he could legally control for the better part of the next two decades, he'd stop at nothing to get his hands on that kind of power. Gina had lived under his thumb, and in fear of his fists, for two long years. She wouldn't allow her child to go through that for a second. Even if it meant never seeing her folks or sister again. Though she promised herself that one day, when she was settled and it was safe, she'd find a way to let them know why she'd had to leave. Because they loved her, she knew they'd understand.

Her building was quiet as she approached. No signs of trouble on the sidewalk outside or in the foyer as she darted in and headed for the stairs.

A low rumbling of voices caught her ear before she reached the second floor, and her silent tread faltered midstep. She was accustomed to hearing her neighbors' muffled voices, music and television through the impossibly thin walls, but this particular voice sent a cascade of gooseflesh over her skin. *Tony.*

Gina spun on instinct, fleeing back the way she'd come and sending a stream of continuous prayers into the ether. *Don't let him find us. Don't let Mr. Larkin tell.* Her apartment manager was old but kind, and she suspected he knew she was running from something. There was understanding in his eyes on the day they'd first met, and she was counting on him now.

SHE WOKE HOURS LATER, to the sounds of her phone alarm and a dozen barking dogs. The scent of animals hung in the air. Groggy and stiff from a night on the cot reserved for extralarge breeds, she shook herself back to life and got moving. The receptionist, Heather, would be in soon, along with the volunteers who walked the dogs and cleaned the kitty litter. Sleeping at the shelter wasn't exactly permissible behavior, not that Heather would tattle, but she'd have a ton of questions. And Gina had already told her too much about her past.

She shuffled toward the restroom, rubbing sleep from her eyes, and dragged the go-bag from her locker on the way. Ten minutes later, she was dressed in a change of nondescript clothing, teeth brushed and dark glasses on. A sleek blond wig and gray headscarf added to the completely new look. She grabbed a granola bar from the vending machine to satisfy her grumbling stomach, then headed to the nearby café, desperate for some hot tea and a place to think.

Gina was immediately thankful for the glasses. Gray clouds and rain had given way to a beautiful, clear blue sky and near-blinding sunlight. The crisp mountain air and peaceful smiling faces made it hard to believe she'd really heard what she thought she'd heard the night before.

And hope began to rise in her core.

The café line was long as usual, but always worth it, and Gina fell easily into step at the end. She fished a few ones from her nearly empty wallet and inhaled the sweet aromas wafting through the open door. Four dollars and change would have to cover it today, at least until she got back to her apartment. The bulk of her money was safely hidden in her grandmother's small sewing kit. She'd learned the hard way early on that accessing her bank accounts somehow tipped Tony off to her general location. His money, and his family's influence, had made it nearly impossible to hide this long, but Gina was a quick study, and her baby's future was at stake.

"Chamomile latte," she told the barista when it was finally her turn.

The older woman didn't bother looking up as Gina paid with her crumpled cash, then put the change in an overflowing tip jar.

She could practically taste the warm, foamy drink already. A few sips of her favorite latte would clear her head and bolster her nerve before she made the trip back to her building. Hopefully a chat with Mr. Larkin would put her mind at ease.

"Name?" the woman at the register asked, cup and marker in hand.

"Heather," Gina said, giving the first name that came to mind.

She moved to the other end of the counter to wait on her drink, scanning the busy café for signs of anyone who might be watching. Satisfied she was safe, her gaze rose to a television mounted on the far wall. A breaking-news banner rolled across the screen. The sound was muted, but closed captions were on, and Gina held her breath as she read the gut-clenching words.

Murder in Great Falls… Unknown shooter left one man dead in his home just after 9:00 p.m.

The camera panned wide, bringing her building into view behind the reporter. A body on a gurney was rolled onto the sidewalk, then piloted into a waiting coroner's van.

Her stomach lurched, and she ran to the ladies' room, arriving just in time for her meager breakfast to make a reappearance. Tears welled in her eyes at the possibility it was Mr. Larkin on the gurney. Could it be a coincidence she'd thought Tony was arguing with her building manager last night, and someone was dead this morning? She splashed cold water against her burning face and pressed a wad of damp paper towels to the back of her neck, attempting to pull herself together and stave off the churning in her stomach.

Tony was undeniably a monster, but could he also be a murderer? The fact that she wasn't sure twisted her unsettled middle even more. She had to let the authorities know it was possible she'd unwittingly led an unstable man to her building, and his visit had resulted in someone's death. It was the right thing to do, even if, hopefully, she was wrong.

To be safe, she'd make the call anonymously. On her way out of town.

Resolve gathered inside her and straightened her spine. She'd collect her tea, find out what happened at her building, then make a call to local police, if needed. From there, she'd gather her things and leave. Her heart broke at the thought, but she shoved the emotion away. She'd prepared for this, knowing the day might come. And if she was lucky, no one in this town's sheriff's department had already been bought by Tony or his family. Maybe then, if he was guilty of murder, he would finally be punished.

Gina willed herself to open the bathroom door, a small, naive part of her clinging to the hope it was all just a coincidence. That she'd overreacted last night. Tony wasn't in town, and whoever had been shot at her building had nothing to do with her.

"Heather," the barista called as she stepped into the narrow hall.

The familiar pang of doom skittered over her skin once more, stopping her short. Paranoia and fear were debilitating some days. Stir in her wildly unpredictable pregnancy hormones, and it was a cocktail for disaster. Clearly this was going to be one of those days.

She shook away the panic and forced her feet forward. She had information to glean and a call to make. Possibly another immediate relocation on her schedule.

A familiar laugh stole the air from her lungs.

Tony appeared at the counter, speaking congenially to the cashier in a smooth, practiced tone. His pressed polo shirt, high-end watch, shoes and jeans screamed of wealth and casual confidence. Everything from his expression to his stance was meant to put the cashier at ease. It was the poison he injected before tying someone to his web.

Gina backed up slowly, ducking into an alcove beside the bathroom door.

"Heather?" the barista called again.

Tony's head snapped up this time, his smile fading slightly as he scanned the room.

The cashier said something, and he returned his attention to her, setting a sheet of paper on the counter between them. He smiled, then reluctantly, after another look around the crowded space, left.

Gina's heart thundered against her ribs and in her ears. Fear clenched her chest and gripped her throat. He'd been so close. The barista had been calling her name. *Not my name*, she remembered, thanking her lucky stars for the habit she'd gotten into weeks ago. *Heather's name*.

She returned to the ladies' room and sat on the filthy floor, knees up and head down, forehead resting on her palms as she struggled to calm herself so she could leave.

She counted to five hundred before her heart rate returned to somewhere near normal and she trusted her legs to hold her again.

"Are you okay, honey?" an older woman asked as Gina pushed onto her feet.

"Yes." She forced a bright smile, bracing herself against the wall for support.

The white-haired woman was, shockingly, the first to enter the ladies' room since Gina had slid to the floor.

"Morning sickness," she said, setting a palm against her middle.

The woman's gaze dropped to Gina's stomach, and a smile erased the concern from her face. "It gets easier, dear," she said. "And one day these moments will seem like little more than a dream."

Gina held on to those words as she exited the restroom, taking her now-tepid tea from the counter with shaking hands. She cut through the waiting crowd of patrons, eyes fixed on the counter where a cashier had spoken to Tony at the front of the café. She craned her neck for a look at whatever he'd left there, then gaped as the flyer came into view.

An image of her in Tony's embrace centered the page above bold text that put a bounty on her head.

Missing Person: Gina Ricci
Age: 26
Height: 5'2"
Weight: 145 pounds
Last seen in West Liberty, Kentucky, on August 8, wearing cutoff jean shorts and a red tank top. $5,000 reward for information leading to her recovery.

Chapter Two

Cruz Winchester put his feet on his desk and kicked back to enjoy the banter flowing between his cousins, Derek and Blaze. Derek, Cruz's business partner and fellow private investigator, had a lifelong love of ruffling his younger brother's feathers, and Blaze, a successful detective, had an equally long running habit of letting him.

Cruz tossed and caught a baseball in the air above his head while the pair battled it out over who had chosen the safer infant car seat for their vehicles. Both Blaze and Derek had recently started families, taking their brotherly competition to new and painfully boring heights.

"All right, all right," Cruz interrupted. "You two are killing me. You're both the World's Best Daddy. Now, can we please move on before all this baby talk gets me ovulating?"

Blaze pulled his gaze, reluctantly, from his

older brother and fixed it on Cruz. "I need some help with reconnaissance work on a person of interest in a homicide case in West Liberty."

Derek pressed a palm to his chest, then raised the other, as if he was about to pledge an oath. "I've got this. Whatever you're struggling with, baby brother, I can help."

Blaze cut a droll look in Cruz's direction. "Did you hear that?"

Cruz tossed the ball again, determined to stay out of the drama, but enjoying his front-row seat to the show.

"I could do it myself, if I had more time," Blaze argued. "But I'm working a full caseload right now, and this is important."

Derek waved his raised hand. "I under-stand," he said, theatrically breaking the second word into syllables. "Some investigative work is better left to a professional."

"Get out of here," Blaze said, laughing at the insinuation. "Just get me the information and bill the precinct." He handed his brother a thin manila folder with the West Liberty Police Department logo printed on the front.

Derek flipped immediately through the papers.

Most of the men in Cruz's family were former military and either current or retired law enforcement. Cruz was proud to be the former, with no interest in being the latter. And he was happy being single, unlike his string of cousins, who'd started getting married off faster than he could accept their fancy invitations.

He dropped his feet to the floor and set the ball aside as a woman shaped like Jessica Rabbit's shorter sister caught his attention outside the office's mirrored storefront windows. His mama would smack him for the mental comparison, rest her soul, but...*damn*, he was only human.

His cousins turned to follow his gaze.

"Who's that?" Blaze asked.

"I have no idea," Cruz said, "but I think I just fell in love."

"That's definitely not love you're feeling, buddy," Blaze returned. "Pull it together."

Cruz counted her steps as she drew closer, willing her to come inside. Her head was down, but she turned her face in the direction of their office several times, stealing furtive glances at the mirrored glass between them. Something in her stride and silhouette said she meant business, and he liked that all the more. "Come on in," he whispered. "Let me help you."

Derek snorted. "In your dreams."

Cruz smirked, but Derek wasn't far from the

truth, though Cruz would never admit that out loud. "She's got to be a tourist, right? Maybe visiting a relative or friend for the day." Because he knew most of the women in town, and he didn't recognize her.

She reached for their office door, and pulled it open.

His cousins made equally stupid sounds of shock, then went deadly silent as the woman walked in.

"Hello," Cruz said, popping onto his feet and offering his best ain't-I-handsome? smile. "I'm Cruz Winchester, and this is my partner, Derek. His brother Blaze." He motioned to the other men.

She nodded politely, scanning each of their faces as they were introduced. "Hello," she said, a little unsteadily. Her gaze latched onto the badge at Blaze's hip, and she seemed to shift away by a fraction. She didn't offer her name.

"What can I help you with?" Cruz asked, stepping around to her side of his desk, then leaning casually against it. "Missing pet? Missing loved one? No job is too big or too small," he drawled, putting the full force of his Southern charm behind it.

"If you're having trouble locating loved ones," Derek butted in, "may I suggest the key chains I handed out at Christmas. Show the lady, Blaze," he suggested.

Blaze spun his keys around one finger, the little square tracker spinning with it. "Normal people use them to find lost keys and cell phones. Derek tracks our family."

The woman's brow furrowed, and a cautious smile curved her lips.

Cruz decided instantly that he'd like to see more of that smile, and moving forward, he'd prefer to be the one who caused it.

"You track your loved ones?" she asked, engaging Derek instead of him.

"Because I care," Derek said, with a bow.

"Derek has boundary issues," his brother said, casting a pointed look at the offender in question, before clapping him on the back, then heading for the door. "Now, I'll never be too lost to be found."

"That's right," Derek called after him. "You're welcome."

Cruz smiled despite himself.

The woman's shoulders relaxed. Either at the bizarre icebreaker, or at Blaze's departure, he couldn't be sure.

"I'm going to go see a man about a horse," Derek said, threading his arms into his jacket, then following in his brother's wake. "Holler if you need me."

She watched him leave too, then turned back to Cruz with expectant eyes.

"He's really on his way to see a man about a horse," Cruz said. "He keeps a stable on his property. Can I get you something to drink?"

"Water?" she asked, a note of hope in her tone.

Cruz motioned to the chair in front of his desk, then went to get a cold bottle from the refrigerator in back.

To his delight, she was seated when he returned. And she'd removed her dark sunglasses, revealing deep brown eyes and impossibly thick lashes. If she'd been a brunette instead of a blonde, he'd have been lost for good. "I didn't catch your name earlier," he said, half-wondering if she planned to tell him anything at all.

She accepted the water, then drank deeply before replacing the cap. "Gina," she said softly, wetting her lips before going on. "Gina Ricci."

The name sounded familiar, but he couldn't quite place it, or decide why she seemed so painfully nervous.

Her rich olive skin contrasted with the platinum hair she'd tucked beneath a headscarf, and he began to wonder about her appearance as a whole. The big glasses. The way she'd stared at Blaze's badge. Maybe she was on the lam.

He returned to his seat, less impressed than he'd been a moment before. "Are you running from someone?" he asked, in a hurry to move this meeting along.

A beat of shock rocked across her pretty face before she quickly flattened her expression. "I'm looking to start over," she said simply, avoiding any sort of answer, which was essentially a yes. "I'm hoping your line of work puts you in contact with the kinds of people who can create fresh identities."

"Fresh identities," he repeated, unimpressed. "You mean fake IDs. Forged papers, that sort of thing?"

She shifted uncomfortably without answering. Another clear yes.

"I'm afraid you've come to the wrong place. My best advice is that you fess up and turn yourself in."

"What?" She frowned a moment, then bristled. "I haven't done anything wrong."

Cruz leaned forward, elbows on the desk and eyes fixed on hers. "If you aren't running from the law, then what are you running from?"

Her back stiffened, and her shoulders squared. "I think it might've been my fault someone was murdered last night. I want to leave town before anyone else gets hurt, but I'm going to need some help with that."

Cruz did his best to cover the shock that came with that declaration. "You're going to have to elaborate," he said, folding his hands on the desk between them. Surely she was confused, or just plain wrong. But either way, she had his full attention for more than her beauty now.

She pulled in a long, slow breath, then began to talk.

Ten minutes later, Cruz had a new image of Gina Ricci, a name he now recognized from the missing person case in West Liberty a couple months back. He'd heard about her each time he'd visited Blaze and his other cousin, Lucas, at their police department in the next town. Cruz had assumed the worst when she hadn't turned up after a few days. Most folks probably had.

Authorities had looked at her boyfriend, Tony Marino, interviewing him as a suspect in her disappearance. Unfortunately for justice, the guy's family owned half the South thanks to a global chain of rural outfitter stores and a proclivity for sound real estate investments. Their wealth and influence had made him practically untouchable. Regardless, there was never any evidence he'd had a clue where she'd gone.

Now Cruz knew why.

GINA WAITED AS Cruz silently processed her story. "Oh," she said, recalling an important detail she'd nearly forgotten. She pulled the missing person flyer from her purse and unfolded it on the desk between them. "Tony left this at the café this morning. It's a small town, and he's put a bounty on me, so that's another problem."

Cruz examined the paper, then lifted his eyes to hers in a tight expression she couldn't quite read. "You're a brunette?"

"Yes," she said, her inflection making it sound more like a question than she'd intended. But, really, how was that possibly relevant? "Well?" she pressed, resting a hand against her twisting stomach. "What do you think?"

He rubbed a palm across the light stubble on his cheeks and chin. "I think you're brave," he said flatly. "Brave to run. Brave to be here now." He worked his jaw, watching her. "Thank you for trusting me with your story. Who else knows?"

"No one," she said, voice cracking slightly on the two little words. "Will you help me?"

Cruz stretched back in his chair, all lean

muscle and confidence. "I can protect you, but I won't help you run. Tony Marino needs to be brought to justice for his crimes. My brother, Knox, is a deputy sheriff here, and my cousins Blaze and Lucas are detectives in your hometown. If you trust me, I can make sure Tony's found and punished to the full extent of the law. Then you can have your old life back, whatever that was before this guy came into it."

Gina's eyes stung and her throat tightened with fresh hope, something she hadn't had in a long while. "Thank you," she said. "I accept." She hadn't dared to ask about his hourly rate or fee, but whatever it was, the cost would be worth it. Even if she needed to take out a massive loan when this was over. Thankfully, she had some savings at her apartment to get him started.

Cruz pulled a packet of paperwork from his drawer and placed it on the desktop beside a pen. "All right. Fill these out, and I'll add you to our client list so we can get started."

She lifted the pen and began to work, hyperaware of his eyes on her, and trying to ignore the jolts of nonsensical attraction flowing through her. She blamed the pregnancy hormones and the fact that she hadn't had any physical contact in months. None. And Gina was a hugger.

It didn't help that Cruz Winchester was unfairly and distractingly attractive. Weren't PIs supposed to be portly, middle-aged drunks? Why did he and his cousins look more like action-movie heroes than actual people? And what must it be like to swim in that gene pool?

The women in Gina's family were short, busty and pear shaped, with thick, unruly hair. She'd learned to work those things to her advantage when she was younger, but even on her best days, she couldn't pull off Cruz's just-stepped-out-of-the-shower look.

"Finished," she said, turning the completed paperwork back to him, and hoping he couldn't somehow read her mind.

He looked through the pages and grinned, then offered her a hand to shake. "Well, Ms. Ricci," Cruz said, "looks like I'm officially at your service."

Chapter Three

Gina watched as Cruz looked over her paperwork with a furrowed brow. "You're a chef?"

"Sous-chef," she corrected. "I was. Now I work at the animal rescue, matching people with their future furry best friends." She tried to smile, but couldn't quite manage the task. Discussing everything she'd been through, and all she'd lost in the process, had raised her anxiety levels to new heights.

He hitched one sandy brow. "Remind me to ask how that works later."

"It's on the website," she said, nervously nibbling her lip. "I've enjoyed my work at the rescue as much as working in any restaurant. Maybe more. Cooking came naturally to me, because I grew up in a kitchen," she rambled. "I'm from this big Italian family, and we're always gathered in the kitchen. Cooking. Eating. Talking." A lump rose in her throat at the memories and she stopped. Cruz didn't care about her past. He was here to fix her future. To do a job. "Sorry." She cleared her throat, dislodging the lump, then setting her fluttering hands back in her lap, another thing she'd picked up from her family. Her mother loved to swing her hands when she spoke, and her sister had a way of getting her whole body involved when the story was good. They were all a little excitable, and she loved it. She missed it. Blending into the walls was depressing, like wearing a too-tight bodysuit that had constricted her heart, mind and lungs.

Cruz watched her, silently, with sharp, ethereal eyes. Was the color even real? He didn't seem the sort to wear contacts, but she'd never seen anything like them before, a barely there hint of green, practically illuminated by his golden tan. How much time did he spend in the sun? And doing what? "I'm more of a grill man myself," he said, apparently making small talk. "What do you cook?"

"Um…" She pulled herself back to the strange conversation, likely intended to put her at ease. "Everything," she said. "And all the time. At my parents' house, we love one another with food. We're probably all carrying an extra five or ten pounds of pasta and pancetta alone."

His gaze left her face for the briefest of moments, snapping instantly back to meet her eyes. "And you like working with animals?"

"Sometimes more than people," she admitted with a small, but honest, smile.

He nodded again, as if he might understand that concept. "When is your baby due?"

"Five months."

He gave her paperwork another quick look. "Your family doesn't know?"

"No one knows."

"And you were going to have your child on the run?" he asked. "Raise it alone while trusting no one and watching your back every second?"

Her chin tipped up in response. "If that's what it took." She hadn't made clear plans for the birth or childcare yet, but she'd been working on it. Her doctor had assured her she'd do all she could to protect her anonymity during checkups, but Gina would have to give her real name to be admitted for delivery, and labor could take hours. Even in the best situation, she'd be stuck overnight, a virtual sitting duck. Plenty of time for Tony to find her, especially if he had a private detective looking for her, which she suspected he might.

Tony was mean and manipulative, but he was only one person. To keep up the chase on his own, while maintaining the facade of brokenhearted boyfriend and working at his family's company, he'd need help. Paid help that he could control. He'd told her once that people in the worst situations were the most useful to him, because they were money motivated and cash loyal.

Gina scanned the framed photos on Cruz's desk, hoping he couldn't be bought. There was an image of him with Derek on the sidewalk outside their office, pointing at the Now Open sign. Another featured Cruz with a group of strangers in fatigues beside a military helicopter. Pictures of other inexplicably handsome men of every age, holding the hands of their wives and children, or carrying babies in their arms. Her tension loosened at the sight. "Are you close to your family, Detective?"

"Cruz," he corrected. "And you have no idea." His cheek twitched on one side, as if there was a hidden joke in there somewhere. "Here's how this is going to work," he said, seamlessly changing the subject. "We're going to be partners, so we can get the job done faster. Sound good?"

Sooner definitely sounded better than later. It was the other part that concerned her. "Partners?" Didn't private investigators work alone? And what help could she offer him in return? She'd already told him everything she knew, and she'd written most of it down in the paperwork. Along with half her life story and the complete contact information for her entire family.

"Yep." He stood and stretched his back, before hooking broad palms against the narrow V of his torso. "Now that we've got the contract out of the way, I'm going to need three things from you."

She felt her eyes narrow. "What things?"

"First, never lie to me," he said. "I ask a lot of questions, so if I overstep or ask you something you think is none of my business, say so, but don't lie. I can't help you if you lie, and before we run into this, withholding information is also a lie."

"Okay." She lifted her hands, then dropped them in her lap. Telling the truth was kind of her thing. She was an oversharer by nature and by nurture, usually to a fault.

He worked his jaw, probably thinking she'd agreed too easily, and not quite believing her.

"Seriously," she said, one hand jumping uselessly up again. "I promise. The whole truth, all the time. Whatever I can do to help."

"All right. Second, you have to trust me," he said, crossing his arms and widening his stance. "I can understand why this one will be tough for you, and I saw the way you looked at Blaze's badge earlier, but my family is good to the core, and we're great at what we do. The Winchesters are also deeply woven into law enforcement around here. You might not want to trust them, but you're going to have to trust me. Because we're working with local authorities on this."

Gina bit the insides of her cheeks. He was right: it wouldn't be easy, but she had to trust someone. At least the cocky PI before her was up-front about who he was and what he expected. In those ways, she supposed, he was already being honest with her. "Okay."

"Great." He clapped his hands, then grabbed his coat off the back of his chair. "Let's go see what we can find out at your building."

She stood and followed, a little off-balance by his announcement of their partnership and subsequent demands. "What's the third thing?" she asked, certain she shouldn't go anywhere with him until all his conditions had been stated.

Cruz pushed the door open with one long arm and held it for her to pass. "Try not to fall in love with me," he said smugly as she moved through the narrow frame. His body heat and cologne clogged her brain momentarily, and she arrived on the sidewalk with an awkward laugh.

"I'll do my best."

"That's all I ask." His returning smile made her laugh again. "I'm going to get you your old life back," he promised. "You made a good choice, visiting my office today."

Gina's smile widened, and she hoped more than anything he was right.

Cruz stopped at a new white Jeep with big tires, no top and no doors.

"Your ride is missing half its parts," she said, stalling while she figured out how to climb into it without looking like a child at the playground.

"Are you okay over there?" he asked, sliding onto the driver's seat. "Or do you need a hand?"

"I can get in," she said, reaching reluctantly for the roll bar to haul herself up. "I'm pregnant, not helpless."

"You're also four-foot-ten. I can get you a step ladder if you need one."

"I am five foot two and a half, thank you very much." She pulled herself into the Jeep and reached for the seat belt. "And I'm not some dainty little daisy."

"I doubt anyone would accuse you of that," he said, smiling as he gunned the engine to life.

And she was sure they were going to get along.

CRUZ PARKED BEHIND Gina's building to avoid prying eyes, then waited while she used her key to access the back door.

Crime scene tape stretched across a large section of the first-floor hallway, and he heard Gina gasp at the sight of it.

"We're in luck," he said over his shoulder, leading her toward the deputy surveying the scene inside the open apartment. "Find anything good?"

His little brother, Knox, turned with a frown that bled easily into a smile. He offered Cruz a fist bump in greeting. "How'd you get in here? And why?" he asked. "Derek said you were at the office fawning over some potential client."

Cruz sucked his teeth to stifle a groan, then took a big step to the side. "I'm here helping Ms. Ricci," he said, revealing the pint-size woman behind him. "Daisy, meet my brother, Deputy Winchester. Knox, Daisy."

Gina gave him a dirty look. "My name is Gina," she said. "I specifically told your brother I am not a daisy."

Knox's lips quirked, fighting a smile. "Cruz thinks he's funny."

"I'm hilarious," Cruz corrected.

A moment later, Knox's gaze hardened on Gina, and recognition lit. "Gina Ricci," he said. "You're the woman from the flyers turning up all over town. You went missing in West Liberty three months ago."

"Two," she corrected, setting a protective hand on her barely there bump.

Knox took notice, then raised a confused look to Cruz. "You found her?"

"I found him," Gina corrected, stepping up to Cruz's side. "I'm the client you mentioned earlier, and I was never missing. Not like you think. Was Mr. Larkin the…victim…last night?" Her voice cracked, and she cleared her throat as she turned toward the open door. The answer was obvious, assuming that was Mr. Larkin's apartment, but she waited for Knox's response anyway.

"We aren't releasing the name of the deceased publicly until we've contacted the next of kin," Knox said, in a perfect show of rote memorization and terribly canned speeches.

"She knows whose apartment that is," Cruz said. "Everyone in this building knows who died, which means the whole town does too by now."

Gina batted her eyes, then touched the pads of her fingers to the corners where tears tried to fall. "Mr. Larkin's wife passed away twelve years ago, and his only son is serving in the military. Navy, I think. There's a photo of him on the desk."

Knox nodded. "We're on it, but it will take some time to reach him."

"So it was him," she said breathlessly but resolved.

Cruz cocked his head and smiled at his brother's stunned expression. "I'll let her fill you in," he said. "She tells it better."

Gina gave Knox the wiki version of her situation, including enough details for him to understand why she and Cruz were there, and why she needed his help. She didn't, however, tell him everything she'd shared with Cruz, and the difference felt unreasonably good.

He waved goodbye to his brother as she led the way to her third-floor apartment, planning to collect her things. Slight splintering around the jamb sent his senses on alert, and his arm bobbed up like a parking garage gate. "Hold up."

He listened before drawing his sidearm and toeing the barrier open.

The entire tiny apartment was mostly visible from the threshold, and obviously ransacked.

"Wait here." Cruz moved quickly through the three small rooms, confirming there weren't any hidden bad guys in a closet or behind the shower curtain. "Clear," he said, returning his handgun to its holster.

Gina stood in the doorway where he'd left

her, obviously crestfallen as she surveyed the damage. "When I saw him at the café, I told myself he might just be passing through. Going town to town distributing flyers. Maybe chasing leads from people who responded to the older posters. I even let myself hope that last night's shooting was unrelated. A terribly timed coincidence. But I can't ignore this." She kicked a plastic cup out of the way as she trudged through the space. "I really liked it in Great Falls."

Cruz snapped a few photos, then texted them to his brother. "Knox has already processed the apartment, dusting for prints and looking for evidence."

"Tony wouldn't leave prints." Gina said, opening a cupboard with canned goods and boxed foods. "He's not stupid. And I…" Her voice trailed to a whisper as her gaze snapped briefly to the open door. Likely she was thinking of the murder scene elsewhere in her building. "I need to get out of town."

She rifled through the nonperishables as Cruz took more photos. "I can pay you for your time so far," she said. "Then the police can take it from here. Maybe they'll even slow him enough to give me a head start this time. At least your brother seems like someone who can't be bought. Maybe the authorities will give a damn, now that Tony's finally killed someone."

She dropped her arms to her sides, hands fisted, and she growled.

"Let me help you," Cruz said, snapping on a pair of plastic gloves, then righting a lamp and overturned table. "What can I do?"

"I need to find my grandmother's sewing tin, then I can leave. The apartment came furnished, so I just need my clothes, toiletries and that tin." She searched through a pile of plastic containers on her countertop. "I can repack and be out in an hour. The food and everything else can stay for the next tenant."

Cruz wasn't sure if she was asking him to help her or planning out loud to sort her thoughts, but she definitely wasn't leaving town alone again.

"Tony killed Mr. Larkin, didn't he?" she asked suddenly, turning somber eyes on him. "I know the whole thing is under investigation, but given the things we're certain of, he did it. Didn't he?"

"Probably," Cruz said.

She nodded, expression unreadable. "I keep wondering if Mr. Larkin told him which apartment was mine, then Tony killed him to silence him. Or if Mr. Larkin tried to protect me, and Tony killed him for his refusal to give in. Either way, Tony found me, maybe through the files in Mr. Larkin's office, and either way, it's incredibly sad and unfair that a man lost his life because of me." She pulled in a deep, shuddered breath, and bit her quivering bottom lip.

Cruz piled unbroken plates into the sink, then tossed broken ones into the trash. "You can't do that."

"Do what?" she croaked, looking as if she might like to scream.

"Blame yourself," he said. "You haven't done anything wrong."

She rolled her eyes, then turned away, back to picking through the mess in her tiny kitchen.

"I'm right about this," he said. "Just so you know."

Gina spun on him, cheeks red, and frustration burning in her eyes. "Really? Because Tony is only in this town because I'm here. He only spoke to Mr. Larkin because I live in this building. Do you know what the only common denominator is there?"

Cruz shrugged, and Gina narrowed her eyes like an angry bunny. "Tony," he said. "You ran because of Tony, and he's hunting you because he's unhinged. Unless you're telling me you have some kind of mind control over this guy. If that's true, why not tell him to stop bothering you, so you can get back to your family and friends?"

"Obviously I can't control him," she snapped, digging more wildly through the mess scattered across her floor. "That's the problem."

"Well, it's one or the other," Cruz argued. "Either you control him, and this is your fault, or he does what he wants, and you had nothing to do with it."

Gina dropped onto her hands and knees and looked under the stove.

"What are you doing?" Cruz asked, returning several things to her cupboards.

"I can't find my grandma's sewing tin," she said. "It's small, like the ones mints sometimes come in. It's trimmed in blue and has a flower and ribbon on the front. I kept it up there, with the canned goods, inside an empty mac-and-cheese box."

Cruz finished cleaning the counter, then began lifting things from the floor while Gina moved on to looking under the refrigerator. When the kitchen was cleaned, he moved on to the living room, appraising the details for the first time.

Gina's apartment was officially the emptiest, saddest place he'd ever visited. There weren't any personal effects or keepsakes anywhere.

No photos or art on the walls. Only a simple white comforter and sheets on an ancient-looking twin bed. Food in one cupboard. And a set of dishes and hand-me-down furniture that came with the place.

A small whimper turned him around with a jolt. "What's wrong?" he asked, instinctively. *Besides the obvious.*

"It's gone," Gina said, jaw clenched and a single tear on her cheek. "Tony found it, and he took it."

"The tin?" Cruz asked, closing the distance between them on autopilot. Sure, it had belonged to her grandmother, but if that was the worst thing that came from this day, he'd consider it a win.

"All my money was in that tin," she said, face going red, and limbs beginning to tremble. "He didn't need it. He took it so I wouldn't have it. So I'd be trapped." A soft sound bubbled out of her, and she came at Cruz, arms wide and wrapping herself around his middle. She pressed her cheek to his torso and squeezed.

Cruz froze, arms outstretched at his sides like a kid pretending to be an airplane.

"I can't pay you now," she said. "I can't run. I can't even call a car service to take me out of town. I spent the last of the money in my purse on a chamomile latte." She groaned, then pushed away as he curled his arms awkwardly over her. "Sorry," she said, lifting her chin and wiping her cheeks. "I'm okay now. I shouldn't have done that. It won't happen again."

He blinked, caught off guard by her unexpected attack hug, and equally unsettled by her sudden absence. "It's fine," he said, sounding and feeling like an idiot. Typically clients didn't attach themselves to him. Aside from his auntie, no one actually hugged him anymore. And he hadn't realized he missed it.

He frowned at the confusing notion.

"Oh, no," Gina said, winding narrow arms around her middle. "No, no, no, no."

"What?" Could it get worse than a psycho tracking her down, killing her building manager and stealing all her money?

Gina slumped onto the ratty sofa, her beautiful skin going pale. "My ultrasound photo was in that tin."

Chapter Four

Cruz righted the toppled chair and small table, then set the couch back on its feet while Gina pulled herself together. It was evident she hated feeling weak, and probably didn't want his help straightening her apartment, but she also needed time to process. Anyone would. And he needed to get his head around the level of danger that had landed in his lap.

A beautiful woman came to him looking for ways to hide from her ex-boyfriend. The woman turned out to be someone believed missing, not a runaway. Now the ex was possibly a murderer, thief and vandalizer.

If Cruz was upset by all that, how must Gina feel?

He dared a look in her direction.

Her horrified expression had turned to resolve. Her shoulders were squared, and her chin had lifted. One palm lay protectively against her middle. She'd been alone, afraid, on the run and pregnant.

Cruz couldn't begin to imagine what that must be like.

He dragged her mattress and box spring back onto the bed frame, then worked the sheets on top. His gaze flickered back to the woman who'd caught his eye outside the office window, and had needed him more than he could've imagined. The weight of her reality was a steamroller to the chest. Had the monster hurt her? Was that why she'd run?

Cruz hadn't taken the time to wonder why she'd initially left home, at least not in terms of specifics. But now that the possibility Tony had physically abused her occurred to him, Cruz was sure he'd enjoy the opportunity to let Tony see what it felt like to be pushed around, frightened and outmatched.

The thought curled his hands into fists and sent fire through his veins. There were all kinds of low-life people in the world, but men who hurt women and children were the worst. That was another reason Cruz had never considered law enforcement as a career. He didn't have the patience of his brother or cousins, and he wouldn't be able to calmly tend to domestic disputes where someone had been terrifying a loved one. Hunting down adulterers and run-of-the-mill criminals was bad enough. Some days Cruz didn't even want to do that, but it was always worth it when justice was served.

Gina stood and returned to her kitchen, then silently loaded the ancient dishwasher. The movements were stiff and robotic. Her previously astute gaze, distant.

"Hey," he said, making his way to her side.

She raised cautious eyes to his, then closed the appliance door.

Cruz stopped a respectable distance away and opened his arms.

Her eyes glossed, and she came immediately to him. This time, he didn't leave her hanging. She sobbed quietly against his shirt, her small body shaking slightly. "I can't believe Mr. Larkin is dead," she whispered. "He protected me. He gave me someplace to live when no one else would. He didn't care that I couldn't provide him with more than a fake name and cash to cover the rent. He just said, 'Welcome.' In return for his kindness, he's murdered."

Cruz rested his cheek against the top of her head and held her firmly, willing to stay that way as long as she needed. "We're going to find and stop him," Cruz vowed. "I'll keep you safe until we do."

She backed away at that, expression guarded and wary. She wiped a tear from her cheek.

"I didn't realize how much I'd missed being hugged." An embarrassed smile played on her lips. "It's been a long time. My family is made of huggers. Talkers. Friends." Her mood elevated slightly at the mention of her family, then she deflated again with a sigh, leaning against the countertop. "I can't believe he found me. I was so careful."

"He didn't find you." Cruz shoved his hands into his back pocket to keep from reaching for her again. "He found your apartment. He can have that."

She rolled her eyes up to meet his. "I'm literally homeless now. I can't even rent a room at a hotel because he took my money. I had to keep it here, because when I opened a bank account in the first town I tried to settle in, he found me within days. Since then, I've relied on cash. Now that's gone. He just keeps taking everything."

"Not anymore," Cruz said. "You did the right thing by coming into my office today. This is where it ends for him. My family's a lot more than just abundant good looks and charm." He winked to ease the tension, then rejoiced when she offered a brief smile.

"He's smart too," she warned. "Conniving and manipulative. Dangerous." She swallowed, then took a moment before going on. "He likes to control people, and when he can't…he can be brutal. And now he knows about the baby."

Cruz's gaze slid to her middle. She hadn't told Tony he was going to be a father. If that didn't tell Cruz everything he needed to know about the kind of monster Tony was, nothing would. He pressed the heel of his hand to his chest, where an uncomfortable shift had taken place. His protective instincts were triggered back at his office, when she'd told her story, but holding her had sent those same feelings into overdrive. The way she'd latched onto him without warning earlier, and the way she'd held him again just now, had knotted everything in his core. And he wasn't sure what that meant.

She rubbed a narrow hand against her forehead. "What am I going to do?"

Cruz shook off the unsettling feeling and moved his hand from his chest to his hip. "For starters, you're coming home with me. My place is safe. You can rest and recuperate while Derek, Blaze and I find this guy."

Her eyes widened, then snapped up to meet his. "I can't do that," she said. "I can't even afford to pay you now. I certainly can't let you give me a place to stay. I'll figure something out."

Cruz crossed his arms. "You're scared, in obvious danger, pregnant and homeless. I know we've just met, but what kind of person do you think I am?"

She shrugged, crestfallen once more. "You seem nice, but people aren't always what they seem."

He wanted to argue that he was much more than nice, but decided to run with it instead. "How nice would I be if I set you loose and wished you luck right now? You're being hunted. I can't turn you away any sooner than you would do that to someone else. Imagine what my auntie would say. You want me to disappoint Auntie?"

She pressed her lips tight, and Cruz could practically see her weighing the impossible options. Keep running, alone, broke and homeless, or stay with a man she'd just met. The last man she'd gone home with had turned out to be a killer. Gina wrapped both arms around her waist, highlighting the weak spot he'd overlooked before.

"Do it for your baby," he said. "Come back to my place with me. Get a good night's sleep for the first time in months. A hot shower. A home-cooked meal. Then you can work on an alternative plan while I help law enforcement find and apprehend Tony. My auntie and sisters-in-law will have anything you need, if anything else is missing here, and they're all a text away."

Her lips parted and her brows rose. "I wouldn't dream of bothering anyone else."

Cruz laughed. "Well, you clearly haven't met my family."

She swallowed, then blushed. "I don't know."

"Gina," he said, enjoying the sound of her name on his tongue, and drawing her eyes back to his. "If you won't come home with me, then let me set you up somewhere. I'll pay, then set up shop outside the place and keep watch. I don't mind that, but it's the weaker option, because if I'm staking out your new digs, I'm not chasing leads on Tony. It puts Derek and the local sheriff's department one man down."

She sunk her teeth into her bottom lip as she considered his offers. "I miss my family."

"Do they know where you are?"

"No." She shook her head. "They know I can't tell them."

"But they know you left intentionally?"

"I think so. I didn't tell them outright, so they couldn't be held accountable for the knowledge, but they should know I'd never leave if I didn't have to. They know how much they mean to me."

Cruz ran a heavy hand over his hair. His family would lose their minds if one of their members vanished, especially one of the women. Statistically speaking, missing women didn't come home, and their reasons for leaving were never good. He made a mental note to get a message safely to Gina's family. They should know she was okay, and that she was with a family who could end this for her. Their contact information was on her paperwork in his office.

"Okay," she said, locking her eyes on his. "I will accept your help, for my baby's sake. I'll stay at your house. I don't want to cause you more work, or do anything to prolong the hunt for Tony. Plus, I intend to see that you're paid for your time on this case. There's no need to add a hotel bill on top of that, and hotels have too many points of entry to monitor with any sort of success."

Cruz chuckled and rubbed his palms together, eager to drop her at his place and get started on tracking Tony. "Very true, and you've made an excellent choice."

"I have one condition," she said.

An unintentional grin spread across his face as he crossed his arms and widened his stance. "All right. Let's hear it."

"I want to help however I can. You have to keep me updated on what you're doing to find him and the progress. I know him. Probably better than anyone, and I can help you if you let me. If you don't, he'll get the best of you. Tony doesn't play by any manual of ethics or honor. You'll underestimate him, and you'll lose."

Cruz clenched his jaw, hating Tony impossibly more every second. "Hey, all I want is to save the day," he said, hoping to sound more cocky than irritated. He dropped his hands to his sides and leaned against the counter with her, trying to look harmless and trustworthy to a woman who had to be scared beyond measure.

"A man with a hero complex," she said, a gentle tease in her tone. "How refreshing."

"You say that like it's a bad thing. What's wrong with a hero complex?" he asked, leaving her side to finish making the bed.

"Well, for starters, it makes me a damsel in distress, and I hate that," she said, folding a dish towel and setting it neatly on the counter. "I know it probably looks that way to you, but I'm doing okay."

"Not a damsel," he said, giving her pillow a playful fluff. "A daisy."

"Oh, shut up." She laughed, and the sound was something he immediately needed to hear again.

They worked in companionable silence until everything had been righted inside her temporary home. It wasn't tough considering the modest quarters.

Eventually, Knox made his way upstairs.

He paused at the open door. "Looks better," he said, turning to face Cruz and Gina.

She offered a small wave. "Cruz helped me straighten up."

Knox nodded. "He's like that. May I come in?"

"Oh," she said. "Of course. Sorry."

He smiled politely, then swept his gaze to Cruz. "She can't stay here."

Cruz returned his most blank expression. "You think?"

"We can call Derek's folks," Knox said, turning his eyes from Cruz to Gina. "Our aunt and uncle have plenty of room, and they understand these sorts of things. Our uncle is former law enforcement."

Gina looked to Cruz.

He folded his arms. "I offered her a room at my place."

One of Knox's eyebrows rose.

Cruz matched the expression.

"I don't mind staying with your aunt and uncle," Gina said. "I don't want to do anything that's…" She seemed to struggle for the right word, looked to Knox, then Cruz and blushed.

The heat in her cheeks seemed to travel to

his pants, along with a variety of inappropriate thoughts about making her blush for far better reasons. Then he gave himself a sharp mental slap. Gina was in trouble. She needed him to help her. Not lust after her. Though he wouldn't mind unpacking the possibility of her returned interest in a few weeks when she was safe once more.

Actually, Tony needed to be cuffed and jailed as soon as possible, because Gina was staying at Cruz's place, and he was only human.

Knox made a loop around the space before returning to Gina. "Is anything missing?"

"My grandmother's tin," she said, stealing an embarrassed look at Cruz. "It had all my money in it, and an ultrasound photo. He wasn't supposed to know about the baby."

Knox rocked back on his heels, head bobbing in understanding. "I see. And your ex has a history of violence?"

Cruz braced himself for the answer.

Gina gave a single stiff dip of her chin, and it broke his heart.

He moved back across the space, drawn to her pain and hating his inability to soothe it. He filled a glass with water, then offered it to her and motioned for her to sit.

She easily accepted the suggestion and the offering. "Thank you."

Knox roamed the apartment, looking at the minute details, examining windows and doing his cop thing. "Keep your eyes out when you leave," he warned. "He could be watching the building, waiting for her to come home."

Gina paled.

Cruz moved into her line of sight, locking his gaze with hers. "You're safe." He took a moment to let the words sink in, then flipped his attention to Knox. "Right?"

Knox nodded at Gina. "You're in good hands."

Cruz returned Gina's empty glass to the sink. "Why don't you pack up? We'll take the rest of your things with us so there's no reason to come back. When you leave my place, it will be to go home to your family."

Her bottom lip quivered at his mention of her family, then her posture straightened. She went to the closet and retrieved a set of luggage.

"Are the books yours?" Cruz asked, eyeballing a small row of tattered paperbacks on the windowsill, several of which he also owned. He couldn't imagine a woman on the run toting books, but neither had he ever heard of a furnished apartment including a collection of classics.

A cell phone rang before Gina answered the question.

She stepped back into view from her bathroom, a pile of shampoos and body wash bottles in one arm, the ringing phone in the other. "It's the animal shelter," she said. "I forgot to call and let them know I'm not coming. What do I do?"

Cruz headed in her direction, then took the bottles from her arm. "Tell them you're sick. You need the rest of the week off. By that time, we'll have a better idea of where things stand with Tony."

She tensed at the sound of his name, then turned away to take the call.

Cruz dragged a hand through his hair as Knox approached. "How's this for a morning?"

Knox smirked. "Murder? Breaking and entering? Abusive stalker? Pregnant woman on the run?" he asked. "I hate that it's happening in my town, but at least I know this guy's going down."

Cruz offered his brother his fist. They locked determined gazes as their knuckles gently collided.

"I've got this," Knox said. "You focus on keeping them safe." He tipped his head to Gina where she spoke softly on the phone, one palm set protectively against her abdomen.

"Divide and conquer," Cruz agreed. And he would take his portion of the duties damn seriously.

Gina pocketed her phone and forced a tight smile in their direction. "I have the flu, and will be in touch as soon as I'm feeling better." She rolled her head over each shoulder and gripped the muscles there. "I hate lying to Heather, but telling the truth puts her in danger."

Cruz's chest pinched again for her. "She doesn't know about your situation?"

"Some." Gina gave a tragic smile. "She's the rescue's receptionist, and my only friend in this town, but I try to say as little as possible. She knows enough to understand why I keep to myself outside work."

Knox made a note on the little pad of paper he kept in his back pocket. "I'll make a call to the animal rescue later today."

A deputy appeared in the doorway, his gaze landing on Knox. "Got a minute?"

"On my way," Knox said, casting his gaze from Cruz, to Gina, then back. "Y'all take care. I'll be in touch."

A few short minutes later, Gina collected the line of paperbacks and added them to a duffel bag in her hand. "This is everything."

Cruz offered his most encouraging smile.

"Then I suppose it's time for us to kick stones." He collected her meager belongings and headed for the door, giving her the space and time to say goodbye if needed.

She passed him on the steps to the lobby. "I hope you're sure about this."

He smiled as he watched her go, because he'd never been so sure about anything in his life.

Chapter Five

An hour later, Gina and Cruz were finally on their way out of town. She clutched her purse to her lap as he pulled his Jeep away from the PI office, where he'd stopped to handle a few things and make it known he wouldn't be back for the rest of the day. Gina had stood near the windows, watching the people outside and hoping Tony wouldn't get the same idea she had and come inside to ask how a person on the run might best hide.

Getting back in the Jeep and out of town had been the only thing she could think of as she'd waited. But now, as the city limits sign flew past, and stretches of homes and shops became fields and forest, she'd begun to wonder if her terrible instincts about men had simply moved her from one dangerous situation to another. What if Cruz Winchester was a monster too?

She stole a careful look in his direction. What did Cruz keep hidden under that unbelievable face and playful disposition? She'd been enamored by Tony's looks and confidence in the beginning, and where had that gotten her?

"How much farther?" she asked, taking mental notes of road signs and landmarks in case her instincts were wrong about the man beside her.

"About five miles," he said. His pale green eyes lowered to where she'd unwittingly moved her hand to her middle, guarding the child she hadn't planned, but would do anything to protect.

"Okay," she said, feigning bravery and suspecting Cruz could see right through the false bravado. "I know it's early, but it's been a long day." And she hadn't rested well on the cot at the animal rescue.

She turned her eyes back to the road, imagining Tony shrinking in their dust, and hoping Cruz was the man he presented himself to be. Her cell phone rang, and she started, then stared briefly at the screen. "It's work again," she said, tucking windblown platinum locks behind her ears.

"They're probably just checking in on you," he assured. "Maybe to see if you need anything. It's getting close to lunchtime."

Gina stared at the phone, not ready to tell

more half-truths, but also not wanting to worry her boss or friend. She forced herself to answer as the device began its fourth ring. "Hello?"

"Gina?" Heather asked. "Where are you?"

She cringed. The wild rush of wind through her phone's speaker was probably a dead giveaway. Gina wasn't home sick or in bed. "Running to the drug store," she fibbed. "Is everything okay?"

She felt Cruz's eyes on her as she waited for Heather's answer.

"No," her friend said. "Not at all." Her hushed tone set Gina's nerves further on edge.

"What happened?"

"A man was just in here asking about you," Heather whispered.

"Who?" Gina felt her stomach tighten, hoping the man had been Knox, not Tony. "Wait," she quickly added, then lowered the phone and pressed the speaker button so Cruz could listen too. "Sorry. Go on."

"I don't know. He had a flyer," Heather said. "He said you're a missing person. The flyer's got your picture on it," she said, her voice falling to a frantic whisper. "And you're with him in the photo. Someone in town recognized you and told him you work here. I said that wasn't true, but he wants me to hang the flyer in the window. I don't want to do it. It feels like putting a target on your back. But if I don't do what he asked, I'm afraid he'll wonder why." Heather made a small hiccup sound. "Gina, I'm afraid I screwed up, and I don't know what to do. Is this about that crazy guy you dated? Was that him?"

Gina wet her lips, heart racing and thoughts churning. Knowing Tony had tossed her empty apartment was one thing. Knowing he'd likely killed her building manager, then gone to confront her friend was enough to make her physically ill. She hated the desperation and panic in Heather's voice, and hated knowing she had inadvertently caused it. "You did the right thing by taking the flyer," she said, with as much confidence and comfort as she could manage. "You should hang the flyer and forget everything I told you about my ex. I'm fine. I'm not the one in the photo. Okay?"

"It sure looked like you," she said. The metallic jangling of keys registered through the line. "And that guy said you went missing less than a month before you turned up here. Listen, I'm heading out for lunch. I was going to stop by, but since you're not home, I think we should meet and get our stories straight in case he comes back. And I know this is absolutely ridiculous to say, but please tell me this has nothing to do with what happened at your building. The news is saying someone is dead. What on earth is happening in this town?"

Gina looked to Cruz for strength, then set her resolve to protect Heather's safety, if not her feelings. "I can't meet you," she said, letting her voice go hard and cold. "I'm not feeling well. I'm picking up a prescription, and I'm going home to my mama's house for chicken soup and rest. That wasn't me on the poster," she repeated. "I'll be back at work as soon as I can."

"Oh," Heather said, sounding confused. Hopefully believing Gina's lies. "Hi. Um…is everything okay?" she asked. Her voice was odd, and seemed to be directed to someone else.

Gina slid her eyes to Cruz, who looked to her as well. The fine hairs on her arms and the back of her neck rose to attention. "Who's there? What's wrong?"

"I put the poster up," Heather said. "I hope you find your girlfriend. Is there something else I can help you with?"

The Jeep nosedived as Cruz traded the gas pedal for the brake. He checked his mirror and pulled the steering wheel in one smooth sequence of actions, executing a perfect U-turn on the empty country road. He tapped the phone app on his dashboard and instructed the device to call the Great Falls Sheriff's Department.

"Heather?" Gina pressed. "Say something to let me know you're okay. Are you still at the rescue?"

Heather's scream was brief but bloodcurdling, and followed by the heavy sound of breaths against the speaker.

"Heather?" she repeated, her voice coming small and cracked. "Heather!"

Cruz barked orders in the background against the beating wind and Gina's ringing ears.

A familiar growl lifted through the phone's speaker, refocusing her attention on the device in her hand. "Hello, Gina," Tony said, his voice cruel and self-satisfied.

Emotions welled, then overflowed in her heart and head. The barely pent-up anger unleashed without her bidding. "What did you do?" She screamed the question, body trembling. "I hate you. You know that. Just let me go! Stop following me. Stop haunting me. Stop hurting people!"

"You're angry," he said. "So am I. And you know how this goes. We fight. Then we make up. But you don't get to leave me!" The final words rattled her phone's speaker and released tears from her eyes. She imagined his beet-red face and the strings of spittle that flew from his lips when he was like this. Usually, she was within striking distance, and her muscles tensed in anticipation of the pain that wouldn't come.

In the background, Heather whimpered and pleaded to be released.

Her friend had taken her place.

"Come back here now," Tony ordered, "or I'll fight with her instead. Then she and I can make up too."

Gina's already roiling stomach heaved, and she hung her head over the space where a door should've been as the glass of water she'd consumed made a reappearance. She pushed the length of her cheap wig away from her face and panted as her pulse settled. "Don't," she said, her fire extinguished by fear. "I'm coming," she said. "You can let her go. I'm sorry."

"Good girl," Tony said. "But I'm going to hold on to your friend until you get here. Then we'll make the exchange. And for the record, it doesn't matter if you want me or not," he said. "You have something of mine now, and I want it back."

The call disconnected and Gina sobbed, wrapping both arms around her torso and her baby.

A hand landed on her shoulder, and she screamed.

"Hey." Cruz's voice boomed in the air. "Gina." He lowered his hand between them, then made a show of opening it, fingers splayed, not fisted, before returning it to the wheel. "I didn't mean to scare you. Knox and another deputy are on their way to the shelter. Your friend won't be alone for long, and Tony will have some explaining to do. You just tell my brother everything you can about that call when we get there, and about any other time he's threatened or hurt you."

Gina bit her lip against a rush of ugly, painful memories, and wondered where she should begin. Then she sent up a silent prayer for Heather's safety and Tony's capture. Maybe he'd finally gone too far, gotten too cocky and would be taken down from his high horse in handcuffs.

Sirens cried in the distance as downtown came back into view.

Gina breathed a little easier, thankful for the perfect storm of luck and timing. The call coming when Cruz was near. Knox moving quickly into action. Heather would be shaken, but at least she would be safe, and Tony would get what was coming to him. Not even his family's money and influence could save him from a murder charge.

The streets were packed with emergency vehicles and lookie-loos as Cruz slid the Jeep into position behind an ambulance. Gina leaped down and met Cruz at the front of the vehicle.

"Doing all right?" he asked.

She nodded, scanning the cluster of men and women in uniform as they spilled in and out of the alley beside the shelter.

Cruz showed her his hand, the way he had in the Jeep, then waited for her to meet his gaze. He moved his arm slowly behind her and set his palm tentatively on her back. "Okay?" he asked, without breaking eye contact. "So you know I'm right here. No matter what's happening over there." He lifted his chin to indicate the alleyway.

She nodded. "Thank you."

Something flashed in his expression at her acceptance, there and gone, too quickly to read. She let him lead her into the mix.

Uniformed deputies nodded as they approached, apparently recognizing Cruz.

Knox hovered near a set of EMTs raising a gurney onto its wheels.

Her heart quickened at the possibility Tony had been shot. Shamefully, she didn't hate the idea if it meant he'd finally been stopped and would be held accountable for his actions when he healed.

Cruz nudged her toward the rough brick wall of the shelter, clearing a path for the EMTs and gurney. But it was Heather's slack face that appeared as they passed. An oxygen mask covered her nose and mouth. Blood-soaked bandages had been applied to her forehead.

Gina's breath caught and her teeth began to chatter as misplaced adrenaline combined with panic in her veins. This was all her fault. She shouldn't have told Heather about Tony. If she hadn't known the truth, this wouldn't have happened. Gina had known better than to let anyone in, and she'd done it anyway.

Cruz's steadying fingertips pressed against her back. "Let's talk to Knox." He ushered her forward once more, and she craned her neck to watch the EMTs load Heather into the ambulance, eyes closed and body still.

"What happened to her?" she asked Knox, voice cracking. "Will she be okay? Where's Tony? What did he do?"

Knox shifted, keen eyes busily scanning the scene around them before landing on Gina. "She was alone and unconscious when we got here. Blunt force trauma to the head. The assailant probably heard the sirens. Her car's been vandalized, and she hasn't woken up."

Air whooshed from Gina's lungs as she followed his gaze to Heather's car, parked farther
down the alley.

Three jagged words had been carved into
the paint.

Come Home Gina.

Chapter Six

Cruz turned to face Gina, tipping forward and speaking low and calmly into her ear. "Let's get out of here so Knox and his team can work," he said. He attempted to block as much of the scene around them as possible, but doubted the effort did much to comfort her.

"Okay." She nodded, then raised her hand to clutch on to his elbow.

The warmth of her acceptance tugged at his chest, and he covered her fingers with his.

Together, they moved away, her gaze on the ground, and his seeking Tony Marino in the crowd. He didn't see him there today, but Cruz wouldn't stop searching until he was found.

Back in the Jeep, Cruz took the most roundabout route home he could manage, making sure no one had followed him from town. For the first time since purchasing the Jeep, he wished he'd kept the top and doors on. Suddenly, the full exposure that normally felt so freeing seemed incredibly reckless, and he longed to get Gina indoors and out of sight.

He caught glimpses of her as they rode silently toward his home. She didn't ask about the route, despite the fact that it was completely different than the way they'd gone before. She must've noticed. Little else seemed to escape her. He couldn't help wondering why she didn't question him. In fact, the longer her silence stretched, the more questions he had.

They took the final turn onto his long gravel driveway at a crawl.

"My house is at the back of the property," he said. "It's visible after we round the bend."

She turned a strained expression his way. "You live in the woods?"

"I live beyond the grove of trees," he corrected with a smile. "They're nice for privacy."

Gina didn't smile back. Probably second-guessing her decision to go home with a stranger.

He could hardly blame her, and after what they'd seen in the alley, he wouldn't be surprised if she locked herself in a room once they were inside. Just in case.

He refreshed his smile. "I take it you lived in the city before? Not a country girl?" Suddenly, he wished he'd paid closer attention to the missing person posters and news briefings when she'd first gone underground. He didn't know the first thing about who she was before her life went south, and if he didn't know her, how was he supposed to make her feel comfortable?

"Yes," she said quietly. "I grew up in an older neighborhood near downtown. Lots of houses and people. Always plenty of kids to play with when I was young and hang out with when I got older." Her lips twitched, almost managing a smile. "My family practically absorbs other families. They pull folks into their orbit and keep them there, an ever-expanding family of loved ones. The More The Merrier is practically our family motto."

Cruz snorted. "Sounds like our families would get along. Maybe they could join ranks and take over Kentucky."

She smiled, but didn't respond.

Cruz supposed he must seem like the lesser of two evils to her at the moment. He just needed to convince her to stick with that line of thinking, rather than get the idea to trade him off for the devil she knew. Something told him that if Tony persisted, she'd eventually return to him just to stop him from hurting anyone else. He could only hope the need to protect her baby would erase that notion from her head, if it ever tried taking root.

He parked the Jeep in front of his home, a small, two-bedroom cottage on three acres, complete with a pond and room for expansion.

"This is your house?" Gina asked.

He turned his eyes to the home's exterior and tried to imagine what she saw there.

Weathered gray shakes. Black roof, door and shutters. White trim. Black mulch, lots of flowers, thanks to his aunt, the family's unofficial gardener, and a red rocker on the front porch beside a garden gnome with a hand-painted sign announcing, Welcome Gnome. Courtesy of his neighbor's daughter, who'd thought the little guy was hilarious and brought him to Cruz's place last month. He'd hung the tire swing in his oak tree for his cousins' kids last year, though they were all a little young for it just yet. The place seemed like a normal house to him. "Yeah. Why?"

Gina's smile slowly appeared. Her gaze slid over the porch, flagstone walkway and bushes. "Nothing. It's nice."

He narrowed his eyes. "What's that mean?"

She shrugged, her lips fighting another grin. "It's just that you're…" She waved a hand in front of him. "You know."

"Ruggedly handsome," he said, filling in her blank. "Go on."

She rolled her eyes, but her smile widened.

"Plus the Jeep. The PI business. The law enforcement family."

He beamed. "So you do think I'm handsome."

She shook her head. "There's clearly nothing wrong with your self-esteem."

"True," he agreed. "What's that have to do with my house?"

She tipped her head over one shoulder and frowned. "I guess I expected a log cabin or some rustic, manly abode."

"My house is manly."

Her smile widened, but she didn't argue. "Your house looks like a fairytale cottage."

His frown deepened. "No, it doesn't."

She laughed, and his heart gave a sturdy kick. "It's lovely. Just not what I expected."

Cruz climbed the steps and unlocked the door, supposing he might've gone the extra mile in making his house feel like a home, but what was wrong with that? His mama had been too busy making ends meet to bother with the appearance of their home, and he'd intentionally put in the extra effort when it was his turn. "Let me show you around."

Much like her apartment, the bulk of his space was visible from the door. An open-concept living room bled into a nook with small dinette. An island separated the kitchen and living space. A hall led to the bedrooms and bath.

"The house needed to be thoroughly gutted when I bought it," he said. "The price was right, regardless, and I was more interested in the land than the structure. I'd originally decided to renovate a little, just enough so I could live on the property while I built something else. But I got attached." He stole a look at Gina to gauge her response.

She scanned the space around them, seeming to take it all in. Her eyes swept to meet his when he didn't go on.

Cruz ignored the thrumming of his heart, and kept talking. "There were notches on doorjambs, marking a child's growth, and hearts with initials circa the early 1900s, carved into the wooden studs when I replaced the damaged drywall." The restoration work had given him respite when he'd first returned from the military, a place to clear his mind and busy his hands. He'd needed both badly. "I couldn't leave it unfinished, and once it was all redone, I liked it too much to build anything else." As an added bonus, there was enough work to do on the grounds to provide a solid excuse for dodging family invitations anytime he preferred a quiet night alone.

He took her on the two-cent tour, watching her expressions closely and attempting to monitor her comfort level. He wanted to ask her what she thought of his home, and reassure her she was safe there, but he also didn't want to push.

Finally, they stopped outside his spare bedroom door. "You'll be my first guest to stay in here." He waved an arm, encouraging her to go inside. "Make yourself at home. I'll grab your things from the Jeep."

He dawdled outside, allowing her the space and time to get comfortable in his home. He returned several minutes later with everything she owned.

She looked up when he stopped in the doorway to her room. "When you said you've never had an overnight guest in here, you meant in this room specifically?" she asked. Her cheeks pinked, and Cruz smiled at the apparent direction of her thoughts. Gina had been thinking about his overnight guests.

A handful of nice women with excellent taste in men flashed through his mind, and he smiled unintentionally. No, his overnight guests typically didn't stay in the guest room.

Gina sat abruptly on the bed. "I hope my presence won't cramp your style," she teased.

"Not at all." He leaned against the doorjamb and crossed his legs at the ankles. "When my dates get here, we typically go straight to my room, so you can have the rest of the house to yourself."

Her mouth opened and eyes widened. She finally cracked a smile when she noticed his. "You're terrible."

"At least now I know what you think of me," he said. "I plan to prove you wrong, by the way. Now, do you want to lie down for a while, or are you hungry? 'Cause I've got a steak in the fridge that's calling my name."

Gina raised a hand to her platinum hair, then peeled off a wig, using her fingers to let down and comb the dark wavy locks hidden beneath.

Cruz did his best not to moan. Brunettes were his downfall, and Gina had the whole package, from the dark chestnut eyes and olive skin to the curves his dreams were made of.

"Care if I take a shower?" she asked.

His lips parted and he had to work them shut. "No." He tipped his head to the hallway, then led her to the bathroom. "Towels and washcloths are in here," he said, opening a built-in cabinet. "Shampoos and soaps are on the edge of the tub. If you need anything else, just holler."

"Thanks. I brought everything I own," she said with a sigh and a laugh.

Cruz offered a small smile in return. "I'll

call Knox and try to get an update on your friend while you shower," he promised.

"Thank you," she said. "For everything."

Cruz dipped his chin in answer, his chest tightening as he looked into her eyes. "You're done running," he promised. "I'm going to see to that."

He'd never meant anything more in his life.

Chapter Seven

Cruz gave up on sleep when the first shafts of sunlight climbed his windowpane and the nearest neighbor's rooster crowed in the distance. Cruz had only been under the covers about three hours, and sleep had come in fits and bursts. He'd stayed up researching Tony Marino and his family, then fallen into bed exhausted, only to remember Gina was across the hall.

The fatigue hadn't lasted.

Instead, his thoughts had wandered into the gutter and stayed there, despite his best efforts to be a mental gentleman. In hindsight, all possibilities of sleep had probably gone straight out the window the moment he'd heard his shower kick on shortly after her arrival. He'd known she was naked then, and it had taken a shot of whiskey and stern internal scolding to push the parade of unbidden images from his mind. The efforts had been mostly successful, at least until he'd gotten into bed.

Having Gina in his house made things a lot harder than he'd expected.

He'd initially pulled himself together by going outside to make dinner on the grill, but she'd padded barefoot onto the deck, her long dark hair hanging in damp waves against her shoulders. Her skin had been pink from the heat and steam of the water, then pebbled when the wind blew.

He groaned and scrubbed a hand over his eyes at the memory, trying to unsee the image that had returned to him a dozen times throughout the night. Her cotton sleep shorts rode low on her hips, exposing a tiny ribbon of flesh above them. The T-shirt had clung to her tantalizing curves.

"Nope," he announced to the empty room, pushing onto his feet. "Uh-uh."

Gina needed a protector, and Cruz was determined to be that man for her. To make her feel safe, and to keep her that way as well. Which meant he had to stay focused.

He considered pumping up the AC, then offering her one of his parkas, but hiding her figure wouldn't stop the attraction. If only he was that lucky. Somehow, in the short time since they'd met, he'd become oddly attached to the woman who was short on height and big on everything that mattered, like honor, courage and heart. He admired her bravery and her tenacity, and marveled at the way she'd left everything she loved behind in an effort to protect her baby. She'd given up her home, her family, her support network and her access to money. She'd left with only what she could carry. And she'd survived. On her own and on the run.

Cruz had enjoyed listening to her talk about her parents and sister over dinner. And the way she'd curled onto the couch with him afterward, when he'd grabbed his laptop to do some research on the Marinos. She could've chosen to sit in his recliner or taken a seat closer to the fireplace, but she'd sat beside him, her legs tucked beneath her and the scent of her vanilla body lotion driving him utterly insane. He hadn't been sure if she'd simply craved the company after so many days spent alone, or the security of being near someone who could physically protect her in case Tony showed up unexpectedly. Cruz wanted to think she might be attracted to him the way he was to her, but being pregnant and on the run from a murderous ex was probably all she could think about.

He forced his sluggish limbs to carry him to the shower, then into the kitchen for coffee. His phone rang as he started a pot of coffee and considered making breakfast. Staying busy helped him think, and making breakfast seemed the most hospitable act he could manage at the awful hour. He raised the phone to his ear. "Winchester."

"Hey," his partner and cousin, Derek, replied. "How's your client?"

"Sleeping," Cruz said, resting his backside against the counter and focusing on whatever news Derek might have to offer. "Learn anything new?"

"Not much," Derek said, sounding almost as tired as Cruz felt. "I'm digging into social media this morning. I spent yesterday flashing a photo of Tony around town, and I plan to get back out there after breakfast."

Cruz smiled. Derek was the king of repetitive, frustrating tasks. He'd keep up the campaign until he had the information they needed, or spoke to every human in Great Falls. "Anyone recognize him?"

"Everyone recognized him," Derek said, breaking the first word into syllables. "Tony was not shy with those flyers, and the locals all bought his story. He's got the whole shopping district on the lookout for her, and missing person posters in half the shop windows. I had to set at least a hundred people straight. I turned it around and told them Tony's the person of interest. I handed out my business card and directed anyone who saw him again to call me or the sheriff's department immediately. I told them not to confront him because he's believed to be dangerous."

Cruz's smile grew. "Smart. Have you heard anything about the receptionist's condition?" he asked.

"No. I've got a nurse contact at the hospital who's going to text me if Heather wakes or has any visitors."

"Good." Cruz nodded. "I looked into Tony's family last night. Gina said they were connected and influential, and she wasn't kidding. Tony's dad owns a chain of outdoor sportsman shops that are spreading across the Midwest. Apparently the Marinos aren't just rich. They're big-game hunters, trackers and gun enthusiasts, doing regular business with shooting galleries and archery ranges."

Derek made a disapproving noise. "So our guy's likely been raised on a steady diet of testosterone and marksmanship."

"That's what I'm thinking," Cruz said. Not exactly the skill set he preferred in an opponent, and the worst possible for Gina's stalker.

"Thankfully, he's not the only one," Derek said.

Cruz's smile returned. The Winchester

men had all been raised by a former lawman, trained by the U.S. military and were completely lethal, though none resorted to any force greater than was absolutely necessary for attaining their goals. Cruz's dad had been aggressive for other reasons, and often without reason, but thankfully, he hadn't stuck around long. His uncle, Derek, Blaze and Lucas's dad, had stepped in to fill the vacant role. Now Cruz and Derek regularly tracked and occasionally apprehended criminals. Their brothers and cousins made arrests. The laws of the state of Kentucky determined the punishments.

"Did you find any previous arrests on file?" Derek asked. "What kind of a record does Tony have?"

Tension gripped Cruz's shoulders, and he pinched the bridge of his nose. "That's another point of concern. There were four previous allegations of domestic violence and stalking against him, but none of them amounted to anything. The first case occurred during his senior year of high school. He was eighteen and the girl was sixteen. Her name was redacted, and the charges were quickly dropped. Three more cases were opened during his stint at a local college. Same results."

"Always makes me wonder how many more

victims there were," Derek said. "How many didn't tell?"

Cruz grunted. He'd thought the same thing. Only a small percentage of abused women ever came forward. Probably because the offenders too often got away. And Tony Marino was one of them. "I hate these guys." He poured a cup of coffee from the finished pot and let his thoughts run over the details he'd gained through Tony's file. "He's got a lengthy list of smaller infringements, from traffic violations for excessive speed and running red lights to illegal gambling and shoplifting."

"The richest ones always think they're above the law," Derek said, the sound of a car engine humming to life on his side of the line. "Why is that?"

Cruz smiled. "Don't know. I've never been rich." He opened the fridge, pulled out a carton of eggs and a pile of veggies. "I suppose it's entitlement, or maybe this guy's just a run-of-the-mill sociopath."

What kind of person murdered an old man one night, then waltzed around town the next day intentionally interacting with everyone? All so he could locate his next victim. Cruz cringed as the thought presented itself. Gina would not be Tony's next victim. Not on Cruz's watch.

His second line beeped, and he took a look at the cell phone's screen, checking the caller ID. "Hey, Knox is trying to reach me."

"Take the call. I'll see what I can dig up in town today," Derek said.

The cousins disconnected, and Cruz took his brother's call. "Hey. What do you have?" he asked, skipping the customary greeting.

"I'm not sure," Knox said, sounding mildly optimistic. "Maybe nothing."

"Can you be a little less vague?" Cruz asked, taking another long sip of coffee.

"I've got a drunk guy leaving a bar, about a block from Gina's apartment building, around the time of Larkin's death. He parked in the alley behind the building to avoid paying for valet. I guess the bar's lot was full. Anyway, he claims to have seen a man fitting Tony's general physical description leaving the apartment building. He remembers because the man was wearing gloves and wiping his hands on a cloth. He didn't think that made sense."

"That's great," Cruz said, standing taller and feeling distinctly hopeful for the first time since taking the case. "Bring Tony in. Get him in a lineup. See if this guy can identify him."

Knox snorted, probably thinking he knew how to do his job without Cruz's help, but Cruz didn't care. Knox needed to move on this. Gina's happiness depended on it. "That's where the problem comes in," Knox said. "This guy laughed through half his statement. He thought he'd imagined it all, and was shocked that I wrote the story down. Especially since he was, and I quote, 'superwasted.' Not my strongest witness, and I don't want to alert Tony and his legal team to start building alibis and a defense case until we've got something more substantial."

Cruz locked his jaw, then cracked a row of eggs into a mixing bowl and beat them until he felt a little better.

"For now," Knox said, "we're collecting facts and leads. There's no way to know what will be important later."

Cruz chopped a trio of mushrooms and a wedge of yellow onion. "Derek's headed back downtown to talk with folks who have Gina's missing person flyer in their shop windows. He's trying to track Tony's movement from the last couple of days." If Cruz was lucky, Derek might even run into Tony. In that case, the jerk would be under arrest by lunchtime.

"Sounds good," Knox agreed. "I'll give Derek a call. I don't want him confronting this guy. Tailing him and letting me know where I can find him is enough."

"Have you had a chance to take a look at Tony's record?" Cruz asked. "The other accusations. The dropped charges."

Knox sighed, long and dramatic. "Sometimes, I think you have the idea I got my badge from one of those claw machines."

"Or a Cracker Jack box," he joked, tossing a bit of pepper into his mouth.

"Of course I looked at his record," Knox said. "I've got contact information on each of his former accusers, and I plan to reach out to them today. I'm shooting for face-to-face encounters, so I can get a read on their eye contact and body language, but one of the women left the state about three weeks after she dropped her charges. I'm going to have to settle for whatever I can get from that one."

"That sounds good." Cruz nodded. Anything they could use to build a case against Tony would be helpful. He added the chopped veggies to the eggs, then poured them into a heated pan. "Keep me posted on your findings. In real time, please."

"You got it," Knox said, agreeing in his usual easy way. He'd always been great about keeping the lines of communication open, something Cruz had been thankful for on more than one occasion.

The thought tightened something brotherly and protective in his chest. "Knox?"

"Yeah?"

"Be careful."

Chapter Eight

The low murmur of a male voice startled Gina awake. Her muscles tensed, and her breaths halted as she opened her eyes to unfamiliar surroundings. It took a moment, and the slow, easy laugh of Cruz Winchester, to bring her up to speed. She wasn't alone in her dinky, lonely apartment, a chair wedged under the doorknob for added protection. She was in the guest room of the sexiest private investigator in Kentucky. Possibly on Earth.

She stretched beneath the butter-soft sheet and inhaled the faint lavender scent of the pillowcase. Then took a long moment to appreciate her complete situation. The past twenty-four hours had been the scariest of her life. A kind man had died and Heather had been hospitalized, both because of Gina, yet she'd stumbled into Cruz Winchester's life. And he'd kept her safe.

He'd gained her full attention at hello, then

he'd taken her under his wing of protection and given her the use of his guest room.

Not to be outdone by the overall adorable appearance of the cottage, her new room was something ripped straight from the pages of a magazine. The curved metal bed frame was dark, as were the wide polished floorboards, but the bedding, curtains and rug were all creamy white. Pale blue designs on an abundance of decorative throw pillows coordinated perfectly with the robin's-egg-blue paint on the walls.

The fluffy down comforter had felt like heaven as she'd pulled it up to her chin the night before, trying hard not to think of her handsome host any more than absolutely necessary. Her emotions were obviously heightened, and her hormones were definitely out of whack. She couldn't afford to get confused about what was happening between her and her protector. She was in danger, and he was doing a job, nothing more. Those deeply interested looks he gave her from time to time, the ones that stole her breath and curled her toes, were probably just him wondering why she was staring at his abs, forearms or lips. A bad habit she'd formed immediately upon meeting him, and one she wasn't sure she could break.

The scents and sounds of breakfast crept

under her door, and she climbed eagerly out of bed. If breakfast was half as good as dinner had been, she never wanted to leave this place.

Gina darted into the bathroom to brush her teeth and hair, then hurried down the hall toward the kitchen.

Cruz stood at the stove in pajama pants and bare feet. Shirtless and glorious, brows furrowed as he reached for the phone on his shoulder. "Be careful," he said before disconnecting and setting the device on the counter.

His gaze jerked to her, as if sensing her arrival, and his lips quirked in a cocky half smile. "Good morning. Sleep well?"

"Morning," she said, more shyly than she'd intended. "I did. Thanks. You?"

He gave a soft laugh, then turned back to the skillet before him. "Not even close," he said, giving his head a little shake. "I hope you're hungry and like omelets. I used some chopped veggies and a handful of cheese. If eggs aren't your thing, I also have fruit and yogurt. Steel-cut oats and granola."

"I like eggs," she said, sliding onto a tall stool at the island behind him. "You certainly eat healthy for a bachelor. I thought single men lived on cold pizza and chicken wings."

He grimaced over his shoulder at her. "Not if I can help it."

Gina stared at the T-shirt lying before her on the granite countertop. A puddle of soft gray fabric she was certain would smell like him if she lifted it to her nose.

Cruz returned his attention to the stove, extinguishing the flame beneath the pan and removing it from the heat. The muscles of his back and shoulders flexed visibly with each twist and lift of his arms.

Gina rested her chin in her palms, enjoying the surge of interest and adrenaline. She normally required two cups of coffee to feel so alert.

"I played ball for a while," he said, picking up the conversation she'd nearly forgotten. "Nutrition was a big part of the required fitness for me."

"What kind of ball?" she asked, suddenly visualizing the body before her as that of an athlete. "Were you any good?"

Cruz turned with two plates of eggs and set them on the island between them. "Baseball, and yes. I was very good."

Her cheeks heated. "I'll bet."

He handed her a fork and napkin, then delivered two glasses with water. "Can I pour you some coffee to go with that?"

"No." She grinned. "I'm good."

"I'll bet," he said, echoing her words, and punctuating them with a wink.

Gina drained half her glass of water before digging into her meal.

Cruz stood across from her while they ate, and she was both thankful and disappointed by the barrier between them.

"Tell me about baseball," she said, genuinely interested in who Cruz had been before he became a private investigator, and trying to imagine the man before her as a high school jock.

His smile grew. "I could hit a home run before I could spell the words," he said, reverence and nostalgia in his tone. "By high school, I was being recruited by a dozen scouts, college and minor league. I had offers for everything from free rides at universities across the country to opportunities other kids in Great Falls, Kentucky, haven't even dreamed of. I thought baseball was my calling. The thing I was destined to do, and something that would change my family's world."

"What happened?" she asked. Obviously, he hadn't become a professional athlete, but why? "An injury?" she guessed.

The wistfulness of Cruz's expression thinned until it looked more painful than positive. "My mom was diagnosed with advanced ovarian cancer. My dad wasn't in the picture, so it was up to Knox and I to keep the lights on when she had to stop working."

"So you gave up the thing you loved most," she said, feeling the tug of his loss in her chest, along with a swell of misplaced pride. "For her."

Cruz pulled his distant gaze back to Gina, fixing her with those soft green eyes. "There's nothing I wouldn't walk away from for family. It wasn't even a choice to be made."

Her hand crossed the island on instinct, covering his before curling her fingers beneath his palm.

He held her gaze, curiosity and something else playing in his soulful eyes. Slowly, he dropped his attention to their joined hands.

Gina released him immediately, understanding she'd crossed a line. "Sorry."

His arm snaked forward to catch her before she could set her hand onto her lap. Long, gentle fingers circled her wrist and gently pulled her hand back to him.

Her eyes widened, and her breath released in a startled pant. She could've broken free with the lightest of tugs, but she didn't want him to let her go.

When his piercing gaze met hers once more, he wet his lips, then set his big, calloused palm on hers, releasing his hold and allowing her to make the next move.

She parted her fingers, sliding them between his. "Do you ever regret leaving baseball?" she asked, desperate to keep him there and talking. She wanted to know more. Anything and everything about him. And she didn't want the strange, charged moment to end.

"No." His voice was thick but confident. "If I'd chosen baseball over Mama, I would've been on the field instead of at her side when she passed, and that is something I could not live with. I don't let people down," he promised.

Gina's eyes stung as the news of his loss reached across the island to her heart. "I'm sorry about your mama."

His phone rang, and they jumped guiltily apart. His eyes were wild, and his expression stunned.

She imagined she looked the same.

Cruz glanced briefly at the phone, then adjusted the waistband of his pajama pants before tugging the T-shirt over his head. "Hello, Auntie," he said, lifting the device to his ear.

Gina finished her water, willing her heated chest and cheeks to cool.

He spoke kindly but quickly, then ended the call a few short moments later and returned to his breakfast. "That was Derek's mama. She's a second mother to Knox and me. She's also a busybody of epic proportions, and she heard I have a woman staying with me. So she wanted to see if she could bring you something."

"Like what?" Gina asked, warmed by the stranger's offer and by the loving way Cruz spoke about his aunt.

He laughed. "Anything you'd like, as long as she can get a look at you. She wants to be sure you're comfortable, happy and doing as well as humanly possible, given your situation."

"I am," Gina said. Her stomach soured, and she pushed her plate away. It was too easy to get lost in the bubble that was Cruz Winchester. Too easy for her to drop her guard. She cleared her throat and straightened her spine. "I don't need anything else, but I'd like to help with your search for Tony however I can. Maybe you can fill me in on what you know so far. I heard you on the phone when I woke."

Cruz patted the counter and nodded. The same curious look returned to his eyes, but he didn't ask her any questions. Instead, he picked up his fork and finished his probably cold breakfast while filling her in on everything she'd missed while she slept.

Gina listened carefully, determined to help.

"I used to keep tabs on him through social media," she said. "The only thing he loves as much as himself is a spotlight." The posts and pictures on his account had given Gina a heads-up on what kind of mood to expect him in most nights. His unpredictable temper had made her thankful for the information on more than one occasion. "I haven't dared log into my accounts since I left home, just in case he has someone watching them. I bought a burner phone and only use the internet at libraries on public terminals." She shook her head and sighed. "I'm sure he can't go long without being the center of attention. Tracking his movements on Instagram would be a good start. Maybe take a look at his parents' Facebook page."

Cruz frowned, an unnatural expression on his typically jovial face. "You can use my laptop whenever you want. I leave it on the coffee table, or my desk if it's charging. I'm always logged in, so you can use my social media accounts to snoop and no one will track you. This is a private network."

She blinked. "Thanks."

Cruz carried their plates and glasses to the sink. "Do you think Tony could be tracking your family online?" he asked.

She considered the answer a moment. "I

don't know," Gina admitted. "I'm not sure what he's capable of, which is why I haven't tried to reach out to them. Why?"

"Because I'd like to talk to your family," he said. "I think Tony knows you're close to your family, so he likely went to them first, hoping to find a lead on your whereabouts. Something he said to them might be helpful to us now. Also," he added, a bit more cautiously, "I'd like to give them an update on you."

"You want to talk to my family?" she asked, a thrill whipping across her skin. She'd give just about anything to see them again, or even to hear their voices. To trade text messages. She hadn't even allowed herself to do that, just in case Tony was somehow monitoring their communication. It was unlikely, and she was admittedly paranoid, but she had everything riding on staying away from him. Her baby depended on it. And she had no doubt that Tony's family could find someone willing to bend to their wishes in exchange for enough cash, no matter where she turned for help.

Except, maybe, the Winchesters.

"Your folks should know that you're okay," Cruz said. "Whatever amount of peace that gives them is worth the risk, and I'll make sure it's a very limited risk. If one of my family members was missing, we'd all be consumed with fears of the worst."

She hated that he was right. Her family was probably beside themselves. "My little sister, Kayla, started school at Bellemont University in West Liberty last fall," she said. "She lives on campus. It's a busy place, and it would make sense for my folks to meet her there from time to time. Maybe we can plan to be there the next time they are," she suggested.

Emotion flooded to the surface as she imagined seeing her family again, of holding them and telling them how much she loved them.

"Let me talk to my cousin Lucas," Cruz said. "He's a detective in West Liberty and a graduate of Bellemont. He might have an idea about where to meet and when. We can send a message to Kayla through him. I'll get dressed and stop by the police station. You can make yourself at home while I'm gone. The security here is better than Camp David. You don't need to worry."

"I won't," Gina said. "Because I'm coming with you."

Chapter Nine

Cruz strode back down the hall toward the living room just after lunch. Lucas had made a morning trip to the Bellemont University campus, something he apparently did on a semiregular basis, and he'd passed a message on to Gina's sister while he was there. The school was within Lucas's jurisdiction, and as a special victims detective, he stayed in contact with campus police. Cruz hadn't given much thought to Lucas's routines before, but he supposed it made perfect sense. Lucas had a deeply personal connection with assault survivors. His wife had been a victim while they'd lived on the Bellemont campus together years ago, before they were married, and her attack was the reason he'd gone into law enforcement. Lucas knew firsthand what attackers took from their victims and their loved ones.

Cruz couldn't imagine working exclusively with those kinds of criminals, but his cousin did it well. "You about ready?" he called to Gina, checking his watch as he arrived in the large open space.

Gina stood near the glass doors in the kitchen, gazing onto the deck, arms wrapped protectively around her middle. This was her most common stance, and it tugged harder at his heart every time he saw it. She probably had no idea she was doing it, or just how often she stood that way, but Cruz had begun to notice everything about her. Knowing she cradled her unborn child as much from fear of a looming monster as from instinctual, maternal love made Cruz tense and anxious. Emotions he'd strictly avoided for years.

She turned to him with a muddled expression of hope and sorrow. "I can't believe I get to see my sister. Are you sure it's really safe?"

Cruz extended an arm in her direction, thankful he could do this for her. "Yeah. I'd hoped to arrange for your folks to be there too, but Lucas thought it was too risky right now. He asked her to hold off on telling your parents for a day or two. If Tony's watching her or them somehow, we don't want to tip our hand. Hopefully you'll see them again soon."

She wiped a tear off her cheek and gave a shaky laugh. "Sorry. Tears of joy, I promise. And I know Kayla will understand. My folks will too, when they eventually find out what's going on."

Cruz smiled, lifted as always by her contagious laugh and beautiful smile. "Don't thank me yet," he said, forcing his cover-up, cocky grin into place. He knew the mask of overt confidence put others at ease. "You're going to need a disguise."

Gina stilled. "Should I grab my wig?"

He pulled a baseball cap from his back pocket and gave it a shake. "I'm not a fan of the wig, and people have seen you in it. Any chance you can get all your hair into this without looking like the gnome my neighbor's kid left on my front porch?"

She laughed. "You have no idea. This is one of my secret skills."

"Wearing a hat?" he asked, smiling sincerely back. "I know infants who can do that."

"You know a lot of infants?" she asked, digging through a handbag she'd dropped near her shoes in the entryway.

"My family is experiencing a baby boom of sorts," he said. "So, yeah. Soon there will be more Winchesters under two than over thirty."

She laughed, then returned the bag to the floor and headed for the hallway. "We haven't had a baby in my family for a decade. Mine will be a total guinea pig for me. I feel a little bad for him or her already."

"I'm sure you'll be great," Cruz said. An image of Gina with a newborn bloomed in his mind, and fresh pressure built in his chest. He shook it off and rolled his shoulders back. He really needed to get a grip, and get his head in the game. Today was a big day, and despite his cousin's assurances about the outing, Cruz was nervous. Potentially putting himself in harm's way wasn't an issue, but unintentionally leading Gina into danger was something he wouldn't soon get over. "How do you feel about wearing one of my jackets?" he asked, projecting his voice in her direction. She could easily blend with the college crowd if she'd stop hugging her middle. Maybe holding her hand would help with that.

"Only if you plan to pin me," she said, returning with a smile. She'd twisted her hair into a tiny knot on top of her head and paused to strike a silly pose.

"How'd you do that?" he asked, genuinely curious as she moved closer. Gina had somehow reduced a mile of thick dark hair into something smaller than his fist and secured it into place.

"About fifteen years of ballet lessons," she said. "I'm the master of the tight bun."

He laughed, brows rising, and her cheeks went red. "Nice."

She laughed again. "Where's the jacket?"

He turned toward the row of hooks on the entryway wall. "Denim or leather?"

She moved to his side and examined her options. Then, she stroked a palm down the sleeve of his favorite brown bomber. "Definitely leather."

Cruz pressed a hand to his chest as she threaded her short arms into his long sleeves. She knew she was killing him, right?

She grinned up at him. "How do I look?"

He groaned and shook his head. She looked like she should be straddling his motorcycle, whipping off that hat and letting her long dark hair fly wild and loose behind her while she wrapped those arms around his waist. "Like you're ready to go," he said, forcing the image out of his head, and telling himself he couldn't actually feel the heat of her hips cradled against his backside, or the weight of her breasts against him, not even her warm breath on his neck.

Yep. She was definitely killing him. Cruz led the way to his Jeep and opened the door for her.

She stopped to look at his freshly reassembled ride. "When did you have time to do this?"

"I took care of it last night," he said, pressing the door shut behind her when she climbed in. There had been no way he was taking her anywhere again without every precaution in place. That included his Jeep's doors and roof. As an added bonus, his windows had a healthy tint to obscure views of her as they drove. He wished he could somehow transport her across campus unseen. His extralarge equipment bag could probably hold her, but he doubted she'd agree to be toted around like a sack of bats and balls. Instead of making the suggestion, he reminded himself that she'd already proved she was tougher than she looked. Whatever happened, she could and would handle it as it came, just as he would. And he'd never been so senselessly proud of someone he had no claim to in his life.

Chapter Ten

Gina held her breath in anticipation as Cruz navigated the pleasant tree-lined roads of Bellemont's beautiful campus. She'd been here once before, when Kayla had come on an official tour as a prospective student. Their dad had been obsessed with security. Their mother fussed over the dining options, and Kayla had been mostly interested in scoping out the student body. Specifically, the guys' bodies. She'd even requested a tour of the gym and pool for this purpose, exactly like the hormone-driven wild card she was. Kayla was everything a little sister should be, carefree, fun loving and generally adored. Gina had always been the dull, quiet, mildly insecure older sister, which, coupled with her comparatively shy nature, had made her the perfect target for Tony's charms and manipulation. If only she had seen that sooner.

"I think this is it," Cruz said, sliding his Jeep into a parking space outside her sister's hall.

She powered her window down by a sliver, enough to let the autumn air seep in without revealing herself to onlookers. Smiling students gathered in groups and clusters on the lawns and walkways between the Jeep and building. Muffled music from portable speakers played beyond the glass. The scene seemed surreal, a view of another world, where Gina's nightmare hadn't yet reached.

"Ready?" Cruz asked.

Gina bit her lip. The thrill of hugging her sister again had been replaced with fear for Kayla's safety on the drive to campus. What if she and Cruz accidentally led Tony to her doorstep? She scanned the smattering of faces in search of him. "What if Tony hired a private investigator like I did?" she asked quietly. "I keep looking for him, but he might have someone else watching Kayla's dorm on his behalf. He has the money, the brains and the motivation. Plus, he can't be everywhere at once."

"I know every PI in the area worth his or her salt," Cruz said. "If one of them sees me with you, they'll call to ask what I was doing here before they report back to him. Professional courtesy." He slid her a confident smile.

"Plus, none of us got into this line of work to wind up on the side of the bad guy."

"Okay, well, what if he hired a friend?" she asked, scanning the unfamiliar faces more closely. "Or paid a student? He told me once that everyone has a price, and the lower the price, the more loyal the ally. College kids are broke, right?"

Cruz's door opened and shut. When she turned back in his direction, he was gone.

A knock on her window caused her to gasp.

Cruz leveled her with a pointed look through the tinted glass. "I wouldn't have brought you here if I didn't believe you and your sister would be safe. Trust me."

A silent war erupted inside her. She believed Cruz was good, honorable and true. She believed he could and would protect her, whatever the personal cost. It seemed to be the very definition of who he was. But the last man she'd trusted...

She growled internally, then jerked open the door, forcing the thought away. Tony was an exception. He was not the rule, and she wouldn't allow him to cause her to fear all men or to believe that he somehow represented the norm. He was a cruel and awful human who would never again control her or her choices.

Cruz jumped clear of the swinging door.

"Well, all right." He smiled. "Love the enthusiasm."

She laughed, feeling lighter as one more link in Tony's chains fell away from her.

Cruz offered his hand. "It's probably best if we walk around like two kids in love instead of a private eye protecting a woman on the run. You know. Just in case."

Gina easily accepted the offer. "I thought there wasn't anything to worry about? No prying eyes, remember?"

Cruz used their joined hands to drag her close, then he released her in favor of sliding his long arm across her back and tucking her against his side. "It's basic due diligence. An extra service I provide at no charge." He turned his face toward hers, and she angled her head back for a better look at him. He was handsome in a way she was never prepared for, and looking up at him from this angle, pressed against his lean, muscled side, engulfed by his warm, spicy scent, she felt her toes curl inside her sneakers.

"Good," she said, forcing a casual smile, "because you're working on a commission basis until Tony's caught. I can't access my bank accounts to pay you before then."

He grinned. "All the more reason to keep you close and safe. If anything bad happens,

I won't get paid." His eyes flashed with mischief as he flexed his fingers against her side. "Cuddle up. We're in love."

She smiled as they began to move toward the dormitory's set of double doors. "You realize we can't get in without a key card, right?"

"Untrue." He turned her back against the exposed brick near one door, then stepped smoothly into her personal space, curving his tall body over hers, until she felt as if they were the only people around. "Is this okay?" he whispered. "If I'm too close, nudge me back."

She rolled her head against the brick. "No. This is fine." She had no idea what he was doing or why, but she wasn't about to object. Her senses were on fire, and the heat in his eyes was slowly melting her bones.

He searched her face for several long beats, as if he might say something of dire importance.

Gina focused on breathing normally and remaining upright, while her body begged her to pant and collapse.

Cruz's gaze relented suddenly, flicking over her head for the barest of seconds before returning to her. "Here we go," he whispered, a look of deep satisfaction lifting his perfect lips.

The glass door opened beside them, and a pair of guys in hoodies and sweat pants darted out.

Cruz snaked a long arm out to catch the door before it closed, then he straightened with a proud smile. "Ladies first."

Gina released a slow, ragged breath, and a small laugh followed. "You're suspiciously adept at that," she said.

"Not my first rodeo." He winked, then looped his arm around her once more. "Lucas said she'd be in the laundry area. We need a key card to access the elevator or stairwells. That would've taken forever."

Gina spotted a sign directing them to the laundry center, then tugged him in that direction, trying not to think too hard or long about how easy it had been to get into the building. "Not how you wanted to spend the rest of the day?"

Cruz slid a peculiar look in her direction, then barked a rugged laugh.

The distinct and familiar squeal of her sister brought Gina's teasing to an end. Her eyes snapped up to see Kayla running at them, arms out and tears falling. She barreled into Gina, and nearly knocked her over. "I can't believe you're really here."

Cruz tightened his hold on Gina, bracing her against the impact. He cleared his throat when Kayla didn't let go. "We should take this reunion somewhere more private," he suggested quietly.

Kayla pulled back. Her gaze rose over Gina's head and her eyes widened. Her mouth opened.

"Kayla, this is Cruz Winchester, the private investigator who's looking after me."

"Shut. Up." Her little sister released her in favor of extending a hand to Cruz. "Was the cop I talked to your brother?" she asked. "You kind of look alike."

"Cousin," Cruz answered, shaking her hand. "I trust he was nice."

Kayla gave a guttural, appreciative chuckle. "Oh, he was very nice." She turned back to Gina. "Have you seen the cousin?"

"Not that one," Gina said. But she had seen Derek and Knox. There was little doubt as to what her sister thought of Lucas, given that he looked like Cruz, even vaguely.

"Ladies," Cruz pressed, tipping his chin to a group of students crisscrossing the area.

Kayla led them to the suite she shared with five other students on the third floor. The roommate who shared her bedroom was thankfully in class. The others were nowhere to be seen. "Sit down and tell me everything immediately," she instructed. "Start with why the hell you ran away." Her sister's initial excitement had slowly settled into something angrier, and more like betrayal as they'd made their way upstairs.

Gina didn't blame her. She'd left without an explanation and would feel exactly the same if their roles were reversed. She also knew Kayla would understand once she'd heard the story.

"Do you have any idea how worried we've been?" Kayla went on, tears pooling in her eyes. "How many people we've spoken to? All the flyers we distributed? We went on the local news, begging whoever took you to bring you back. Mama called a psychic to try to find you. Dad hired a private investigator. They thought they'd found you a week after you left because someone used your bank account, but that was the last thread they found to pull. It was hard. Having the hope yanked away again."

Cruz gave Gina a knowing look. She'd thought Tony had found her when she accessed her bank.

"Dad's PI found me?" Gina asked.

"Yeah." Kayla flopped onto her twin bed, and patted the space beside her until Gina sat too. "Tony went crazy from there. He got his own PI and put him on the hunt. Or at least he said he did, but nothing turned up again. We thought you were dead." Her eyes misted with tears once more. "What have you been doing? And why?" She swung her attention to Cruz.

"Your cousin wouldn't tell me anything, except that Gina was okay and coming to see me. And that I couldn't tell anyone. Not even Mom and Dad." She turned back to Gina with a flabbergasted huff. "What is happening?"

Cruz leaned against the wall beside the door and waited silently while Gina forced the complicated and heartbreaking story through trembling lips.

Kayla's gaze dropped to her sister's middle when she finished. "You're having a baby?"

Gina's eyes heated with unshed tears. "Yeah."

Kayla lunged for her again, pulling her into the tightest, most sisterly hug that her heart could've asked for. "I love it already. I'm going to be its favorite aunt."

Gina laughed. "Looking forward to knowing the gender so you don't keep calling my baby 'it.'"

Cruz snorted.

Kayla laughed. "Sorry. This is all just…a lot. I knew it had something to do with Tony. I hate that guy."

Cruz shifted, head tilting and curious-investigator expression in place. "Why? Did he ever do or say anything that rubbed you the wrong way? Something specific?"

Kayla looked from Cruz to her sister. "We

reached out to your friends after you went missing, and they said you'd pulled away from them months before. I'd had no idea. You came around the house less often, but I didn't realize he was slowly isolating you. I would've shown up at your place every day. Twice if I had to. I realized after talking with your friends that the only time I saw you anymore was when you came over with Tony, and that was when I started to wonder if he was the reason you were gone. I told Mom and Dad, then none of us trusted him. Dad thought Tony might've killed you." She covered her mouth, eyes wide, as if it could've been true.

And it could've.

Gina embraced her little sister once more. The isolation had begun without her even realizing, and the bad experiences with him had escalated from there. "I'm sorry I scared you. I didn't know what else to do. He was angry one night. I don't remember what it was about. Sometimes, I didn't know. I'd just learned about the baby, but hadn't told him, and he choked me." She paused to catch her breath, humiliation scorching her cheeks. Her fingers rose to the tender skin, where she could sometimes still feel his fingers squeezing. The marks had healed weeks ago, but she wasn't over it. She doubted she ever would be. "I panicked," she said. "He'd never done that before, and it hit me. His aggressions were escalating. What would he be like by the time the baby was born? What if he hurt the baby? Or killed me? And my baby would be left in his hands. It was all too much, and I worried that telling anyone would bring his wrath on them too. At first, I only planned to take a couple days to think it over, but he kept calling me. Over and over, straight through the night. Then he somehow tracked me to the Hilton and came into the lobby demanding my room number. I left right after he was thrown out. I learned later that someone pulled the fire alarm and the building was evacuated. I knew he did that to flush me out. Thankfully, I was already gone. So I just kept running. I tried to disappear."

"I heard him yelling at her one night," Kayla said, turning a guilty expression on Cruz. "I told our parents, and they promised to talk to her, but she said it wasn't a big deal. I wondered if I'd been wrong. I thought I was crazy."

Gina gripped her sister's hand. "I'm sorry. I didn't want them to worry. I should've talked to you about it, but I just wanted to forget."

Kayla swung her attention back. "When you disappeared, I blamed myself for not making someone listen when I knew how he'd talked to you."

"This isn't your fault," Gina said, shocked and horrified that Tony's behavior had hurt Kayla too. That she'd shouldered this burden of guilt alone and without cause.

"When Tony came around looking for details, Mom, Dad and I didn't say anything about our suspicions," Kayla said. "We didn't know what to make of him or his potential role in whatever had happened to you. He came over all the time, asking the same questions. When did we last see you? What did you say? Where might you go? His family practically orchestrated a crusade to find you. I think we all wondered if it was for show. If he knew where you were all along because he'd taken you there."

Gina's skin heated with the horror of Tony visiting her family without her as a buffer to his anger. What if he'd lashed out at them? She used to think he kept his internal monster contained, saved only for her displeasure. But after what he'd done to Mr. Larkin and Heather, a new, impossibly scarier image of Tony had taken shape in her mind.

"Hey." Cruz stepped forward, concern on his brow. "Are you okay?" he asked Gina.

She nodded, though it felt a little like an out-of-body experience.

"Do you have any water in there?" he asked Kayla, glancing at her minifridge.

She pulled out two bottles and offered them to him.

He took one, opened it, then passed it to Gina, who accepted on autopilot. "Drink. You look white as a ghost."

Gina put the bottle to her lips out of obligation, trying to be polite, but her thirst came from nowhere. She drank half the bottle without stopping, and came up for air a little breathless.

"Sorry," Kayla said, returning the second bottle to the fridge. "I can't imagine how hard this has been for you. I'm too focused on me. What can I do to help?"

Gina looked at the closed fridge. "Were those Mama's leftover containers I saw in there?"

Kayla frowned, then smiled. "Yeah. Manicotti. Do you want some?" She opened the fridge again and slipped two containers into a bag, then passed it to Cruz. "For later."

His lips quirked and he nodded. "Care if I ask a few questions before we have to go?"

"No," she said. "Please do. I want to help Gina come home. Safely."

"What can you tell me about Tony or his behavior since Gina's been gone?" Cruz asked. "Do you have ideas where I can find him?"

"I don't know where he is now," she said. "But I might have something useful." She turned and opened a drawer in her desk. "I started keeping a log of his behavior on the third day that Gina was gone. Everything I read online said that after three days, the odds of a victim returning are drastically reduced. I kept thinking about his angry voice on the night he yelled at her, and I was sure he'd done something to her. So, I took notes." She passed a folder to Cruz. "I logged every time he showed up at our house, how long he stayed and anything he said or asked that made me uncomfortable. I also clipped newspaper reports with her name and interviews he gave about her."

Cruz flipped through the notebook, head nodding. "This is great. Can I keep it? I'd like to hand it over to my brother. He's the local deputy for the area where Tony's been seen, and where we believe he hurt those people."

"Go for it," she said. "I hope it helps."

Gina squeezed her sister's hand in thanks.

Kayla unhooked a minicanister of pepper spray from her book bag and gave it to Gina. "Before you go." She closed Gina's fingers over the can.

Gina considered telling Kayla she needed the defense spray more than Gina did. She had Cruz after all, but she knew Kayla likely had a drawer full of similar products. Their father would've made sure of that.

Cruz's phone rang a few short minutes later, and the sisters stopped to listen, though it was a brief and mostly one-sided conversation. Cruz smiled as he tucked away his phone.

Hope inflated Gina's heart and goose bumps scattered across her skin. "Good news?"

He nodded. "Knox needs me back in Great Falls," he said. "My informant, Rex, is at the station, and I want to talk to him."

Gina set her empty water bottle aside and gave her sister one last hug. "I love you. Stay safe. And remember not to tell anyone you've heard from me, okay?"

Kayla nodded quickly, her eyes filled with tears once more. "Love you too."

"Nice to meet you, Kayla," Cruz said, opening the door and setting his palm against Gina's back. "Lucas will be in touch. We'll try to work out another visit again soon. Maybe with your folks next time. Until then, watch yourself. Get another pepper spray in your book bag."

Gina warmed impossibly further to him. His thoughtfulness toward her sister's safety meant everything. She waved over her shoulder, unable to say the word *goodbye*.

Cruz wrapped an arm around her shoulders once they were in the hallway, and pulled her in close.

"Protect her," Kayla called after them, her thin voice cracking on the words.

Cruz cast a confident glance over his shoulder, devilish grin in place. "With my life," he said.

And Gina believed he meant it.

Chapter Eleven

Cruz parked in the visitor lot of the Great Falls Sheriff's Department. His skin tingled and his heart pumped hard with anticipation. Rex was an excellent friend to have in the PI business. He saw and heard everything that went on in their town—good, bad and gruesome. He knew all the worst kinds of people, but Rex was one of the good guys. More or less. And he only sought Cruz out when something big was afoot.

According to the recent call from Knox, Rex had dialed Dispatch and requested to be picked up by a cruiser, for appearances' sake. Smart, because thugs, which was what Rex pretended to be most days, rarely walked willingly into the sheriff's department, and Rex had a reputation to uphold. He'd told the deputy who'd taken the call that he wanted Knox to make his faux arrest, and the entire conversation was so bizarre, the deputy had passed the news on to

Knox, assuming it was a joke. Knox had re-routed his cruiser immediately.

Following the flashers-and-handcuffs show, Rex had refused to talk until Cruz was present. The guy had had too many unpleasant, but probably deserved, run-ins with lawmen to believe any of them could see past his rough exterior. So Knox had made the call.

Cruz unbuckled and gave his silent passenger an appraising look.

Gina had been distant since they'd returned to his Jeep. She'd wiped tears discreetly and answered his questions with simple, often one-word answers, and stared out her window without bothering to make eye contact. It was the first time since they'd met that she'd shut him out, and he didn't like it. Even after her friend had been attacked, Gina was open to discussion, ready to be comforted. This was something else completely, and he felt the loss of her communication in his gut.

"Come on," he said, in the most positive tone he could manage. "Maybe Rex has something we can use to speed up the inevitable." He stared at her cheek until she dared a look, then he offered a wink and reassuring smile. "Tony's capture and arrest are inevitable, in case that was unclear."

Her lips quirked in response, but she was

fully deflated, and the half-hearted effort didn't reach her eyes. The light and joy that had filled her in her sister's presence was completely extinguished. What remained was heartbreaking, but she persevered, climbing down and moving in the right direction.

Cruz met her at the front of the Jeep, then he set a hand against her back as they moved toward the station. He watched her for signs he'd crossed a line, but her expression gave nothing away. He told himself that Gina was from a family of huggers, so the physical connection would be a comfort to her, and he ignored the part of himself who knew the touch was selfish. He'd wanted an excuse to regain the connection they'd shared on campus, one that had felt so easy and natural, he'd craved another hit. "This okay?" he asked eventually, assuring he hadn't overstepped.

She nodded. "Thank you." The ragged breath following her words sounded like a release of nerves, and he smiled at the possibility his presence and touch had helped her relax.

Before them, a pair of deputies held the door as Cruz and Gina passed through the glass vestibule. The Great Falls Sheriff's Department was a relatively new redbrick building just outside the more populated downtown area, and a place Cruz visited often.

"Hey, Cruz," the deputy greeted him as he held the door. His partner simply nodded.

Cruz returned the greeting, trying not to eyeball the second deputy, whose attention was fixed on Gina.

Inside the lobby, the man at the desk smiled. "Your brother's waiting for you," he said, buzzing the door to the interior offices unlocked as Cruz and Gina headed that way.

"Thanks," Cruz called.

They passed several more uniformed deputies in the long narrow hall. Each greeted Cruz in words, while their eyes trailed over the woman at his side.

Gina made a small, unfamiliar sound, and he slowed his pace to look at her.

Had she noticed all the interested looks too? Had they made her uncomfortable? "What?" he asked finally, needing to know.

She raised her brows along with her grin. "Is there anyone here who doesn't know you?"

Cruz frowned. "Probably not," he said, confused. That was what had made her laugh? "Small town," he reminded her.

"I live in a small town," she said. "I don't know everyone I pass, and I don't know any police officers."

"Maybe you live in the wrong small town," he suggested, returning her smile. "It helps that my little brother is a deputy here. Plus, Derek and I do work for these guys on occasion."

"There you are." Knox's voice stopped Cruz in his tracks, and Gina froze with him. They backed up a few paces and turned toward an open door on the right. Knox stood behind a small table in a viewing room, waving them inside. "Gina." He nodded.

She waved, then took a seat at the table when Knox did.

Cruz preferred to stand.

Knox switched his gaze from his brother to Gina, then back, deadly serious, just the way he was born. "I wanted to brief you on my progress before you speak with Rex," he said. "I've tried to reach Tony through all the usual means. Home visit. Office visit. A trip to his parents' house. So far, I haven't made contact, and no one at those locations is offering any help. In fact," he said, pausing to shift on his seat, "his mother threatened to call her husband and report me." Knox pursed his lips, expression going comically blank. "She was calling a businessman to report a deputy sheriff. If that doesn't tell us everything we need to know about this family's inflated sense of purpose and power, I'm not sure what would."

"That's the Marinos," Gina said. "They run their world and control everyone in it."

Knox frowned, and concern lined his youthful face. "They run sporting goods stores."

"They have a lot of money and no scruples," she said, voice flat and hard. "They lure you in with appearances, hospitality and pretty views, then they stick you to their web."

Cruz moved close to Gina and leaned a hip against the table, eyes fixed on Knox. "Did you tell his mama or coworkers he's wanted in association with murder and assault?"

"Of course not," Knox said. "I told them I was looking for Gina and hoped he could help."

Gina thunked her elbows on the table and rested her face against her palms.

Cruz's hand landed lightly between her shoulder blades without thought.

Knox tracked the motion with his gaze, curiosity in his keen eyes, then carried on as if nothing was amiss. "We've got to be careful how we approach this," he said. "We don't want to tip our hat to the fact that Gina is in our care and under our protection. He could lash out again. We need a solid case for arrest, and preferably no more innocent victims."

Gina raised her face from her hands, a look of disgust on her pretty face. "'Preferably'?"

Knox nodded. "We can't control Tony until he's in our custody. We can only do our best to find and apprehend him, then hold him on the strongest legs possible. Currently, we don't have any evidence to put him at any of our crime scenes. There's only your testimony to hearing his voice through Heather's phone and behind Larkin's apartment door. That's circumstantial at best. A first-year law student could get him off charges based on that."

Cruz straightened, pulling his hand away from Gina, and stuffed his fingers into the front pocket of his jeans.

Knox stood. "That's all I've got for now. If you're ready for Rex, I'll bring him in." He reached for a remote resting on a ledge in the wall behind him and pointed it at a television mounted in the corner, before walking back into the hall.

The flat-screen illuminated with an image of a room like the one they were in.

"You doing okay?" Cruz asked Gina as the door closed behind Knox.

She took a full breath and nodded. "I'm trying," she said. "But my heart and head are everywhere. If I'm being terrible company, it's me, not you."

Cruz snorted. "It's not you. It's the situation, the uncertainty and a wild card named Tony Marino."

She grimaced. "Who wouldn't be wreaking havoc on this town if not for me."

Cruz groaned, debating the boundaries of his role in her life once more. Giving in to the moment, he crouched at her side, bringing his gaze level with hers. "The way I see it, a lot of people have failed you where Tony is concerned. Not the other way around."

She lifted a sincere but uncertain gaze to him.

"I won't be one of them."

The television drew their attention when the door to the room on-screen opened. Knox led Rex inside and offered him a seat at the small table. Rex sat, and Knox left.

"That's my cue," Cruz said, pushing back onto his feet. "I'm going in there, and Knox will sit with you. You can watch and listen while I talk with Rex."

The door to their room opened, and Knox strode inside. "You're up."

Cruz looked to Gina, who offered a small smile, letting him know she was okay without him, because why wouldn't she be? And he went to see his informant.

Rex looked up when Cruz entered the room. The young man's wary eyes tracked him as he moved. Rex was a good argument for nature over nurture, because no one had ever nurtured

Rex as far as Cruz could see, but the kid still knew how to do the right things.

"You rang?" Cruz asked, offering his hand in the familiar shake they shared. Rex had taught Cruz the set of simple motions when he'd rolled into his life three years ago, after stealing a car the insurance company had tasked Cruz with finding.

Rex had planned to sell the car, or its parts, for cash. It was a harsh winter, and Rex was cold and hungry. His girlfriend had pushed him into the crime because she hadn't wanted to stay at the shelter. She'd claimed someone there had sexually harassed her, and Rex couldn't protect her when the men and women were separated at lights out.

Cruz had returned the car and fed the teens, then put the girlfriend up for a few nights at a hotel until the snowstorms had passed and Rex was bailed out. A bond had formed between them that day, when Rex had realized it was Cruz who'd ponied up the dough and kept his girlfriend safe when he couldn't.

Now, at the ripe old age of nineteen, the young man before him rocked his head back in silent greeting. The girlfriend was long gone, and any debt between the men had long ago been paid, but a friendship had taken root in its place. Rex folded his tattooed hands on the table, amusingly at home, despite his dangerous appearance. "'Bout time you showed your pretty all-American face," he said, a reference to Cruz's high school baseball career. It was something Rex had read about online after looking him up three years ago, trying to decipher Cruz's angle for helping him out. Eventually, he'd realized Cruz was just a good guy, but the baseball detail clearly still amused him. "There's only so much free coffee and doughnuts a guy can handle."

Cruz took the seat across from him and smiled. "Sounds like my brother gave you the royal treatment. He usually makes me get my own water from the fountain."

Rex stretched long jean-clad legs beneath the narrow table, a faint smile playing on his pierced lips. "Yeah, well, he pretended to arrest me first. So there's that."

"He's accommodating too," Cruz said. "Why not just call an Uber?"

"I wouldn't have needed the theatrics if you were at your office."

"I've been busy," Cruz said, nerves zigzagging in his unsettled stomach. "You have news?"

"Yeah. I was lifting some dude's wallet when a rich guy stopped me." He lifted his brows in challenge, daring Cruz to scold or reprimand him, per the usual.

Cruz bit down on the insides of his cheeks, forcing himself to let Rex go on.

"The second guy bumped right into me, knocked me away from my mark before I could get the wallet. I thought it was dumb luck, at first. Then the second guy pulls a Benjamin from his wallet and just holds it out to me, stuck between his two fingers like he's about to smoke a cigarette."

Cruz felt his brows rise. "Someone gave you a hundred dollars after catching you trying to steal a wallet?"

Rex dipped his chin in response. "He said he saw what I was up to, and told me if I needed money, he had a job."

Hair rose on the back of Cruz's neck as he listened, taking in Rex's tone and posture. "What kind of job?"

Rex flicked his gaze to the camera on the wall behind Cruz's head. "He told me to watch the building where that guy was killed, and call this number if I saw the lady from the flyer." Rex rocked onto one hip, extracting Gina's folded missing person flyer from his pocket. A phone number had been scribbled across the top in pen.

Cruz's fingers curled into fists on his lap. "Anything else?"

"I get another hundred every time I call to tell him more about her movement, but I haven't called him," Rex said, leveling Cruz with a pointed stare. "'Cause I saw her with you, which either means you need to know this because you're in the reunion business now, or you need to know this because that guy's no good. Maybe even hunting your lady. She sure didn't look lost when I saw her. So, I don't know what's up with her, but in my experience, a man with money to burn is dangerous."

Heat rushed over Cruz's chest, spreading from his core to his forehead in seconds. "You're right to tell me," he said. "She is in danger, and I'm keeping her safe. That starts with getting my hands on this guy, but so far he's smoke."

Rex nodded solemnly. "I figured. I'll do what I can, but hold on to her tight because I'm not the only one he's paying to find her. And someone else will gladly turn her over for money."

Heat turned to fire on Cruz's skin. "That's not going to happen."

Chapter Twelve

Gina struggled to find her breath as the conversation between Cruz and Rex unfolded onscreen.

"You're okay," Knox said. His deep voice was jarring in the otherwise silent room. "Rex is loyal to Cruz. He's an asset, and the fact that he came here looking for him tells me he's serious about helping us keep you safe."

Her gaze flickered back to the men on camera.

"I've got you," the younger man said, voice low and eyes searching. The deep intention behind the words felt like a pledge of fealty.

The fact that a stranger would willingly insert himself into her mess, based on Cruz's involvement alone, was both humbling and mind-boggling. Gina's family and friends were close, but outside her immediate bloodline, she wasn't sure she knew anyone who'd intentionally put their well-being on the line for her.

The relationships she'd been exposed to since meeting the Winchesters gave her an incredible sense of hope.

Knox's desire to help might've stemmed from his badge, but she got the feeling his reasoning ran much deeper. Same for their cousin Derek. And for Cruz. Now Rex. Was it because their world was so much more dangerous than hers used to be? Maybe living in a constant state of emergency caused people to reevaluate priorities and align themselves more steadfastly to doing the right things.

Maybe truly good people simply had a way of finding one another.

"I saw you and her carrying suitcases away from the building, and I heard her apartment was trashed," Rex said. "This guy's going to know she moved on, and if I don't reach out and report that, I'm either hiding something, or I'm not a very good informant. Either way, I lose cred and he'll cut me loose."

Gina's muscles tightened as Cruz nodded. "So you'll call and let him know she's gone," Cruz said. "He already knows that."

"I can tell him I caught sight of a cleaning service hauling boxes down from her apartment. Then I'll give him the number I saw on their van. Your number or your brother's. When he calls you for information, you can arrange to meet him, or do whatever it is you good guys do."

Cruz stood and freed his wallet from one pocket. He handed Rex a folded set of bills. "Get something to eat. Do not buy weed. Take some food home for later."

"Nah." Rex waved him off. "I don't need your money." He rose to his feet, then met Cruz at the end of the table. "I'm working at Allen's Wrench. Folks are nice. The pay is fair, and they don't even mind my ink."

Cruz's smile was wide and proud. "Well, okay, then." He tucked the money back into his wallet. "I'll have to bring the Jeep around sometime. Get a look at you in action."

Rex looked away, fighting a smile and a blush. His head bobbed. "Yeah, all right."

Cruz pulled him into an awkward man-hug. They patted one another's back, then split ways.

"I'm here for you," Rex said. "Whatever you need."

"I know," Cruz agreed, his voice low and rough. "The guy you're dealing with is dangerous. So be careful."

Rex lifted his chin. "Yeah." He offered Cruz a fist to bump, then reached for the door to leave.

Gina felt her lungs strain and realized she'd

been holding her breath. More and more people were being pulled into her storm, and she absolutely hated it. How had things gotten so out of control? When would the madness end?

Would someone else be hurt in the wake caused by her escape?

Knox's gaze heated her cheek, causing her to steal a look his way. "How are you doing?" he asked.

"I'll be okay," she answered quickly, willing the words to be true.

"You really are safe with Cruz, but if you'd be more comfortable with our aunt and uncle, the offer stands. I spoke to them on the matter again this morning. It won't hurt Cruz's feelings." Knox grinned, and the sudden resemblance to his brother was profound. "Everyone involved only wants you to feel safe. You've been through enough."

She forced a tight smile. "Thank you."

The door to their room opened, and Cruz appeared in the doorway, pale green gaze moving swiftly from Gina to his brother. "You heard all that."

"We did," Knox answered. "It's a good plan, assuming we can get Tony to meet with us, or at least stay on the call long enough to trace it. It'll be a quick sting."

Gina tried and failed to take on a little of the

Winchesters' confidence. It was nice that they looked out for one another, and for Rex. She appreciated the extra step Knox had taken to be sure she was comfortable at Cruz's place too. He was right to ask, because she wouldn't have likely said so if she wasn't happy there, not after Cruz had given her a place to stay when she'd needed it and agreed to take her case, even when she couldn't pay.

An obvious realization settled over her, and she inhaled the freedom that came with it. The time had come for her to stop running and start fighting. She wasn't alone in the battle, and the Winchesters didn't have to be either. Gina needed to switch gears.

Now, if she could just keep her heart and head in line while spending so much time with the man who'd stolen her breath at first sight.

GINA'S STOMACH RUMBLED as she retrieved her mom's manicotti from Cruz's refrigerator. She sent up silent prayers of gratitude for the small portion Kayla had sent home with them. "Mind if I use your oven?" she called to Cruz, giving herself a mental pat on her back for asking. It seemed odd to make herself so comfortable in the home of someone she'd just met, but he'd repeatedly insisted she try. She'd spent so long tiptoeing around Tony's place, even after living there for months, caution had become second nature. Today, however, she was actively reminding herself that Tony was an anomaly, and she couldn't let him darken her view of the world anymore. Despite his every effort to make her feel like something less, she wasn't buying his lies anymore. She wasn't a burden or a hassle. She was Gina Ricci, and she was a dang delight.

"Help yourself to anything you want," Cruz answered from his seat at a desk in his living space. "If you're hungry, I can make dinner."

"I'm heating the manicotti," she said, smiling at her assertion. "Would you like some?"

Cruz stopped typing. He twisted at the waist and hooked an elbow over the back of his chair. "You'd share that with me?"

"You're sharing your entire house with me," she said. "I suppose it's the polite thing to do, but you're getting the smaller piece."

He smiled. "I accept."

Gina transferred their dinner from her mother's plastic containers to a baking dish, then slid the cheese-and-spinach-stuffed pasta sleeves into the preheated oven and set a timer to warm them up. The microwave would've done the work faster, but in Gina's opinion, the oven did a nicer job.

She considered taking a seat at the counter,

or returning to her room until the food was ready, but wandered in Cruz's direction instead. He'd been typing diligently on his laptop since they'd returned from the sheriff's department. She'd forced herself to leave him until now, but curiosity had finally gotten the best of her.

He stilled as she approached, as if he'd heard or sensed her arrival.

"What are you up to?" she asked, determined not to feel as if she was intruding.

Cruz gave his keyboard a few dramatic taps, then turned to face her. "I've established a website for the fictional cleaning service Rex is name-dropping to Tony. I've been texting with Rex, and we decided giving Tony the number was too easy, too suspicious. Instead, Rex will name-drop, then Tony will look for a number on his own. He'll find the number to my unregistered pay-by-month cell phone and give me a call for more information on where I moved the lady in your apartment." He grinned, obviously proud of himself, and clearly not doing something like this for the first time.

"That site looks real," she said, pulling her attention over his shoulder and stooping for a clearer view of the monitor. "You did all that since we got home?"

He shrugged. "I create a lot of cover stories.

I'm getting faster with practice. If you ever need a website, I'm your guy."

Gina laughed. "Good to know."

"I also designed a few ads for the company and set them to run immediately in our town's community forums. The extra effort will make it even easier for him to find me, and help legitimize the front."

"Well, aren't you a man of many talents," she mused. Her cheeks burned a moment later as the comment turned extremely dirty in her mind.

Cruz's eyes twinkled with renewed mischief, obviously picking up on the unintended double entendre and likely her blush. "That I am," he agreed.

A smile broke over Gina's face, and she turned away on her toes. "I'd better go check on dinner."

Cruz followed her into the kitchen, then opened a cupboard for plates. "You want to eat at the island or the table?"

"Island," she said breezily, knowing the chairs there were much more closely spaced.

Inside the oven, the manicotti bubbled slightly, letting her know it was ready. She donned the pair of oven mitts hanging from a hook on the side of his nearby refrigerator, then moved the baking dish to a trivet Cruz had placed on the countertop.

She took her seat beside him, and fell easily into conversation about their already very full day. Gina especially enjoyed Cruz's rehashing of time spent with Kayla. He'd noticed everything from their obvious bond to candid photos of her family hung around her sister's vanity mirror and computer monitor. She shared the stories behind the snapshots and smiled at the memories. "I miss them so much," she admitted.

"I can see," he answered warmly. "I'm working on fixing that."

By the time the manicotti was gone, and Gina was stuffed, Cruz had slipped away to take a call. It was the first time he'd left her to talk on the phone, and her curiosity spiked. What was different about this call?

She considered following him and insisting he keep her in the loop. Except she couldn't be sure the call was about her case, and if it wasn't, she had no right to listen in.

Gina busied herself washing the dishes, then wiping countertops, before pacing the width of his living room until a better idea came to mind.

She crossed the space to the desk where Cruz had worked earlier and borrowed a notepad and pen, then took a seat on his couch to think and write. Just because she wasn't on the run anymore didn't mean she should be a complete bystander. After a couple years spent with Tony, she had to know something that would be useful in finding him, at least indirectly.

She tapped the pen against the paper, then began a list of names. She included everyone she could think of who shared Tony's world, starting with his personal staff. A housekeeper who came weekly. A favorite driver who took him to important events. Friends she'd met at his parties. Frenemies and scorned exes he'd whispered about at galleries and charity dinners. Anyone who might know something more than she did and could be convinced to tell. She considered adding his family members, but Knox was already on that, and the Marinos would never turn on Tony anyway.

Soon, the page before her was full, and the result was a bit of a surprise. Tony was private and guarded, but she'd forgotten how often he was in the spotlight. He might've kept his personal demons tightly under wraps, but a great number of people knew enough about the camera-ready version of Tony to possibly offer local police a little insight. For example, where did the driver and town car take him most often? Where had Tony traveled with the scorned exes? Had he recently requested access to a friend or business cohort's cabin or empty apartment?

She considered the places Tony had taken her, but none were close enough to keep an effective eye on Great Falls. Either he had a new hideout, or he was hiding in plain sight.

Her skin crawled at the thought.

A sharp clap of hands caused her to yip, and nearly leap from the couch.

Cruz parted his clasped hands as he approached, a look of apology on his face. "Sorry." His gaze moved swiftly over her wide-eyed face, to the palm pressed to her chest, then to the borrowed notebook on her lap. "I didn't mean to startle you. I have news, but what's this?"

Gina passed him the notebook while working to regain her composure. "I made a list of everyone I've ever met through Tony. I don't know many last names, but this seemed like it could help. May be a good start for you detective types."

Cruz evaluated the paper, brows raised. "This is more than a start. This is fantastic. Knox and Derek will be thrilled for the added leads." When his gaze returned to hers, something soft and new was there. She wasn't sure, but it seemed a lot like pride.

She averted her eyes a moment before pushing onto her feet and sliding her palms against her middle. "I hope it helps. Now it's your turn. What's the news?"

A slow grin spread over Cruz's face. "I was on the phone with Derek. He's been following your parents all day."

Her muscles stiffened at the mention of her folks. A seed of fear took immediate root. "Why?"

"I asked him to," Cruz said, scanning Gina's stricken face and painfully tense posture. "For you," he clarified. "He's making sure they aren't being watched by anyone else."

"And they aren't?" she asked, feeling her fingers curl against her sides. "Right?"

"No." Delight danced in Cruz's eyes. "Which is why we think it's safe for you to visit them."

Gina's heart leaped. "What?"

"According to you and Kayla, your parents attend mass every week. We thought it would be easiest to slip into the church and meet with them in a private room. They can come and go as usual without drawing any inquiring eyes, in case Derek somehow missed their tail."

Pressure built in Gina's chest, and she threw herself against Cruz, wrapping him in the energy and appreciation she couldn't yet speak.

His strong arms closed around her on a chuckle. "I hoped this might be your reaction. Remind me to always be the one to deliver your good news," he said. "And to provide it as often as possible."

She laughed, then settled into him for a long moment, enjoying the warmth and comfort of his embrace. His heart beat fast and strong beneath her ear, and she wondered if he felt the zigzagging electricity too. If only she could find reasons to hold on to him like this more often.

"There's one more thing," Cruz said quietly, skimming his palms up her spine. "We've been out in the Jeep a couple times already. We should probably mix it up."

She tipped her head back to ask what he had in mind, and the heat of his breath swept over her, knocking her silent instead.

"How do you feel about taking my motorcycle?" he asked.

And every part of her squealed with joy.

Chapter Thirteen

Gina scooted in close to Cruz on the sleek black motorcycle. Her heart hammered as the machine purred beneath them, rocketing over the ribbon of winding country road in the darkness. Her bulbous helmet and mirrored shield gave her an exhilarating feeling of anonymity when rolling fields and scattered farms gave way to clustered downtown buildings and a sea of taillights.

St. Peter's Cathedral rose above all else in the distance. Its majestic spires gleamed white beneath strategically placed floodlights.

A surge of excitement raced through her, knowing her parents were so near. Her limbs tightened in response.

With one large palm, Cruz covered her clasped hands where they lay on his chest, then curled strong fingers over hers. Her galloping heart moved straight to a sprint at the silent encouragement, and she rested her cheek against his back.

Soon, the motorcycle sailed into a narrow employee parking lot behind St. Peter's, and she followed Cruz's lead in dismounting the bike, but leaving her helmet on as they approached the building. She'd been to church with her family a thousand times, but always parked in the visitors' lot out front. She'd never even seen the black metal door where Cruz stopped to knock.

The barrier opened immediately, and someone in a suit and tie ushered them inside.

Gina's heart swelled as the man's face registered. "Mr. Garcia," she whispered, her happy heart beginning to dance at yet another positive piece of her past.

Mr. Garcia had been a friend of her parents for as long as she could remember. He and his wife had even babysat Gina and Kayla when they were young. "Thank you," she whispered.

He offered a warm smile, then greeted Cruz with a handshake and nod. "I invited the Riccis to wait for me in the multipurpose room," he said softly as the muffled sounds of organ music rose in distant parts of the building. A choir of voices and the ashy smell of incense followed. "I told them I wanted to discuss another fundraiser for our affiliated elementary school. I'm quite sure they'll be thrilled to see that was all a ruse." He grinned, and his dark eyes sparkled with pleasure. "We should hurry so you'll have as much time as possible with them." He turned and hurried down the long, narrow hallway with Cruz and Gina on his heels.

"How do you two know each other?" she asked the men, not caring who answered. Was her world really this small?

Cruz set his palm against the small of her back, matching his pace to hers. "We don't."

Mr. Garcia smiled over his shoulder. "I answered the phone when his partner, Derek, called and explained the situation. I happened to be in the office after a meeting with the school's advisory board. The regular office staff had already gone home for the day. It was a perfect alignment of circumstances, really. I caught your parents as soon as I saw them pull into the lot." He paused at the closed door to a large gathering room usually saved for wedding showers and funeral dinners, then offered Cruz a determined look. "If there's anything else I can do to help, just ask."

"Thank you," Cruz said.

Mr. Garcia stepped aside, pretending to fiddle with his phone, probably standing guard as a lookout.

Cruz opened the door, and motioned Gina inside.

Her mother's gasp and sob propelled her across the room and into the embrace she'd needed for months.

"Baby," her mama cooed. The single word was soaked in relief as she buried her face in Gina's hair. "I can't believe it's you." She pulled back to look into her daughter's eyes, a mix of elation and misery on her round face. "We've been so scared. Where have you been? Are you okay?"

Her father hovered, motionless at their sides before wiping heavy hands over his crumbling features.

Gina reached for him, pulling him into their sweet reunion cocoon.

Long minutes passed before the tears and professions of love began to slow.

Cruz stepped in with a box of tissues when Gina's nose began to run. "Maybe we should all have a seat," he suggested, adding a brief introduction of himself before motioning to the nearest round table, large enough to seat eight. "We don't have a lot of time, but there's plenty to say."

Her dad cleared his throat, then led the women to the table. He pulled chairs out for Gina and her mom, then her parents bookended her. Her dad's arm went around her shoulders, and her mama squeezed Gina's hands.

Cruz nodded, and Gina began to tell her story once more. Just as she had for Kayla, and like her sister, her parents cried. Hurt and betrayal registered in their eyes as she explained the truth about Tony and all the things she'd kept from them. They clung to her and to one another, heartbroken, when she admitted she'd felt as if she'd had no other choice than to run.

"We could've helped you," her dad said, voice heavy with despair. "We will always help you. No matter the fight. I thought you understood that, Gina. Always."

Her mother pulled more tissues from the box and dabbed them to her eyes. "I can't believe he hurt you, and we didn't know. Kayla warned us one night when she heard you arguing, but we couldn't believe it was more than a heated dispute. The Marinos are pillars of the community, and Tony was always so polite. That family made it their full-time job to find you."

Gina rubbed her mama's arm. "I didn't want to upset you by telling you about the early fights with Tony. By the time he'd become dangerous, I was afraid to get you involved. I can see how wrong I was now, but back then, it was hard to see anything clearly. I'm so sorry."

"Oh." Her mama stroked her hair and pulled

her close. "We do not blame you," she whispered emphatically. "And we don't judge you. You hear that? We would never."

Her dad shifted, unsettled and antsy now. "Do you think his family knew about this? About the things he did to you? About what he's doing now?"

Gina pulled in a ragged breath. She hadn't even told them the worst of it, only that he'd become abusive, and she'd run. She steadied herself with a glance at Cruz for strength, then pushed ahead before she started to cry all over again. "I don't know how much Tony's family knows about who he really is, behind closed doors, but I know they would never turn him in or aid in his arrest. The family isn't what they seem either. They're dark," Gina said, her voice falling unintentionally to a whisper. "I didn't see it until it was already too late, but they're manipulative, always scheming for influence and power in their circles." She dragged her attention from her dad to her mom, then back. "I know you'll always protect me," she said, needing him to understand he hadn't done anything wrong. "You've made that obvious to Kayla and I all our lives, but the world had gotten muddled to me. I was trying to protect you."

Her dad sighed, then pulled her in for another hug before kissing her head. "Let us help you now. We aren't completely useless, you know?" He forced a humorless smile, then raised his eyes to Cruz in question. "What can we do?"

"Dad," she said carefully, drawing his attention to her once more. There was something else they needed to know right away. "There's another reason I ran." Her eyes stung and blurred as she lowered her attention to her hands, now pressed against her abdomen. "I needed to protect my baby."

Her dad covered his mouth, and his gaze jumped to her mother.

"Gina?" her mother asked, turning her back to face her, then wrapping her in another hug.

When she straightened, her dad's eyes glistened as he looked from her face to her middle. "We're going to be grandparents?"

Gina nodded, and her dad pulled her into a hug.

He held her hand when he released her, then turned doubly determined eyes on Cruz. "And your family is looking for Tony?" her dad asked.

"Yes, sir," Cruz returned, taking over while Gina and her mom stole another long hug. "My brother, Knox, is the deputy sheriff assigned to Gina's case," he said, repeating the information Gina had initially dumped on them. "My cousins are detectives in West Liberty, where Gina was first reported missing. They'll oversee things from your town, while Knox keeps watch from mine. My partner, Derek, and I are working with the sheriff's department to protect Gina and her baby while also tracking Tony. So far there hasn't been any word on where he's staying, but the hunt is happening covertly. He's got enough money to run and stay hidden if he knows we're after him. We don't want to tip all our cards yet."

Her dad grunted. "You have enough evidence to arrest him, then? Will Gina need to stand trial? Do convicted domestic assault criminals even get any jail time?"

Gina's heart seized, and she straightened in her seat, locking gazes briefly with Cruz.

"Not often enough," Cruz said. "But murderers do."

"What?" her mother cried.

Cruz pressed onward, providing the ugly details of Mr. Larkin's murder and Heather's attack.

Her dad swore.

Cruz stood, then fished a pair of cell phones from his pocket and handed one to her dad, the other to Gina. "These are unregistered. I've added my name and number in the contacts, as well as all the information you need to reach my brother and cousins. Also, a number for reaching Gina."

Gina clutched the device against her chest, her heart swelling with joy. When had he done this? How long had he been arranging this reunion with her folks? How had she missed it?

Her mother made a small sound of excitement. "Kayla is going to be so jealous."

A little laugh bubbled from Gina's lips. "Thank you," she told Cruz.

He tipped his head forward slightly, in one small but magnanimous move. "You'll be able to keep in touch now, but you can't let anyone else know." He fixed her with his piercing gaze, then shared the look with each of her parents. "Only answer if the incoming number belongs to one of the contacts I've programmed. Unknown numbers get ignored. Always. Understand?"

Her dad's lips parted as he looked from the phone to Cruz. "Yes."

Her mom sighed deeply, audibly relieved. "But we can talk to her?"

"Yeah." Cruz smiled. "A little, and as needed. Otherwise don't deviate from your usual routines. It's evident that you're happier now than when you arrived here tonight. Try not to let that show when you leave this room," he continued. "Given all that's happened with Gina's case in the last few days, we don't want anyone to suspect you know where she is or how to find her."

The door to the room opened, and Mr. Garcia stepped inside, a palm raised in apology. "Sorry," he said. "I didn't want to interrupt, but mass is ending."

Gina's heart sank as her mom's arms wound around her once more.

"I love you, Mama," she whispered, before standing and turning to her dad.

Her father wrapped her tight in the most fatherly of hugs, then kissed the top of her head. He cupped her face in his hands when she started to pull away. "I love you, baby girl."

Suddenly, the hero of her youth seemed more gray and fragile than she'd ever thought him before. "I love you too," she said.

"We'll do everything we can to bring you home safely and soon," he vowed.

"I know." She nodded. "I'm going to be okay," she assured them, meaning it in her marrow.

Her mother moved to her father's side as Gina went to Cruz.

"Protect our little girl," her mom pleaded to Cruz, echoing Kayla's parting words as they headed for the door.

"And our grandbaby," her dad said.

"With my life," Cruz vowed once again.

Then he clutched her hand and towed her away.

Chapter Fourteen

The sprint to his motorcycle gave Gina time to collect herself emotionally. The helmet's mirrored visor hid her puffy eyes as they climbed aboard, and the night enveloped her wholly as they rocketed back through town.

Her mind raced with thanks for the day's reunions and for the phone in her pocket, provided by Cruz. The sexy private investigator was becoming more of a hero with every action. His quiet confidence and easy smile had done more for her in a few days than any love interest ever had, and he probably didn't have a clue. Because he wasn't playing games. He didn't have a side agenda or ulterior motive. Cruz Winchester was sincere and honorable in ways she'd forgotten men could be, and he'd irrevocably changed her ideas about what was acceptable. Never again would she accept any relationship that didn't make her feel secure, seen and valued. Because if a man she'd just met could make her feel like this, then anyone seeking a position in her life permanently would have to bring a serious A game. Not just for her benefit, but for the life she would soon bring into this world.

The bike slowed at the final stoplight at the edge of town. Behind them, the area's nightlife was in full swing. Before them, a quiet country road reached out to carry them home.

A shrill ringing rose from her pocket, barely audible through her helmet and over the sound of the motorcycle's engine. Gina felt Cruz's chest rumble as he chuckled in response.

"We didn't get far," he called.

Gina grinned as she liberated the new phone, then called back to Cruz. "Can I answer?" Her heart leaped, eager to hear her mom's voice again, though it hadn't been more than ten minutes since she'd last said goodbye.

Cruz pulled forward as the light changed and guided the motorcycle into an empty parking lot. He circled away from the security lights and traffic, then settled the engine so she could speak, unfettered by the sound.

She tugged her helmet off and pressed the phone to her ear. "Hello, Mama," she said, brightly. "Everything okay?"

"We're fine," her mama said firmly, sounding as if she wasn't actually sure. "It's probably nothing…" The following pause stretched across their line, hollowing Gina with each impossibly long beat.

"Mama?" she pressed. "What's wrong? Just say it."

"The company monitoring our home security system called. We've had a break-in."

CRUZ PACED HIS living room an hour later, hating the pained expression on Gina's face. The only thing worse than seeing her misery was knowing he'd contributed to it, even a little, by insisting they go back to his place, rather than to her parents' home. She'd wanted to see them after learning about the break-in, but he couldn't allow it, even if it hurt her not to be with them.

Her priority was her family, but his priority was her safety.

So he'd driven her to his place as planned, and though she understood, logically, why she couldn't be with her parents, the pain of not going to them was etched on her face.

His phone buzzed against his palm as he fielded the texts from his cousins Blaze and Lucas. Neither of the detectives typically covered break-ins or missing persons, but they'd had no trouble getting involved when Cruz asked.

The newest text was from his partner. "Derek just arrived," he told Gina, moving to join her on the couch. "Blaze and Lucas have spoken with your folks and confirmed that they are fine. The intruder was long gone when they arrived, and police were already on the scene. I'm sure your mom and dad will call as soon as they can. They're probably just waiting until they're alone again. They know how important it is to keep your reunion a secret."

Gina fixed him with an angry and exasperated stare, cheeks pink from emotion and eyes narrowed. "I hate this so much. I know this happened to them because of me, and it makes me crazy. I left town to keep Tony away from them. I hurt and worried them for months, but I told myself that was okay, because at least they were safe. Now he's closer to finding me than he's ever been, and he circled back to where he started. I haven't protected them at all. I worried them for nothing. Who knows what he'll do next? And there's nothing I can do to help."

Cruz rubbed his palms over the thighs of his jeans, willing himself not to reach for her, and deciding silently that if she reached out to him, the only right thing to do would be to hold her. But it had to be her choice. Her decision. Her move. "You're doing exactly what you should be doing right now," he said.

She nodded, but didn't look convinced. Her gaze slid to the floor, then to her twined fingers, where they rested on her lap.

He hated the waves of guilt and conflict rolling off her, and wished she could see how strong she was. She'd made a brave and selfless choice, despite unthinkable circumstances, and there was honor in that risk, not shame. "You've consistently done the right things, since the day you ran away, and you've made it abundantly clear to Tony that he cannot control you any longer," Cruz said. "He's apparently not accustomed to that, and he's mad."

Gina's frown deepened. "So it was definitely him? No chance of a coincidence?"

"No." Cruz pursed his lips, realizing she'd still held some hope that they were wrong. "According to Blaze, the front door was kicked in. The hutch in the dining room was overturned, and all the dishes inside were destroyed, along with several porcelain figures and an oil painting above the fireplace in the living room." He paused to swallow against the itchy dryness of his throat, when she sucked in an audible breath. "A message was spray-painted in red across the carpet." He waited for her gaze to meet his before adding the final detail. "'Keep hiding. Keep paying.'"

Gina's hands curled into fists. Her jaw

locked and her cheeks darkened. "That was absolutely Tony," she seethed. "Who else would it be? He went straight for my family's most cherished possessions. He wanted to hit us where it hurt."

"The items in the dining room were important?" Cruz guessed, aligning the new information with what he knew about Tony Marino. He was a manipulator and a world-class jerk.

"Everything he destroyed was an heirloom," she said. "The china and figurines came from Italy with my father's family at the turn of the last century. The painting was a portrait of my great-great-grandmother and every bit as old and irreplaceable. What he did was cruel. This wasn't a burglary. It was a punishment."

Cruz stretched onto his feet, then went to the kitchen for two bottles of water. "It sounds counterintuitive, but it wouldn't be all bad news if Tony lost a little control. A plotting, self-poised sociopath is a lot harder to catch and build a case against than one who's lashing out and acting on impulse." He returned to the couch and offered Gina one of the bottles, then opened the other for himself. "But I'm not convinced that's what's happening. More likely, breaking into your parents' place was intended to either draw you out or to produce some details on your location. He went while the house was empty for a reason. He might've sorted through their things, their papers, their computers, if they leave them unlocked."

Gina sipped the water, appearing to consider Cruz's words. She set the bottle aside a moment later, then pulled her feet onto the cushion beneath her. Her eyes rounded and her gaze darted, an indication of rapid, probably unpleasant, thoughts. "What if you're wrong and my family was his target—they just weren't home?"

"I don't think so." Cruz set his nearly empty bottle aside, and sorted through the mash-up of thoughts in his mind. He wanted to console her so desperately, it was complicating his ability to remain strictly logical, and this was new and scary territory.

One of the things that made Cruz an excellent private investigator was his ability to compartmentalize. He separated himself emotionally from the cases, because keeping a clear and objective mind was key. Working with Gina had blown all that out the window, and it was a continuous struggle to keep his eyes on the end goal instead of on her.

"Why?" she asked, forcing him back to the conversation at hand.

"You have to remember that he still doesn't know you're with me, or that the lawmen in two towns are after him. He thinks he's going to get what he wants. So hurting your family isn't in his best interest, because that would ensure you'd never come back," Cruz said. "I think he's still trying to manipulate you, and the break-in at your parents' house was designed to intimidate and motivate you to return to him, if you're still in touch with your family. It's probably also a test to see if you're in contact with them. And I'm sure he did some snooping while he was in there wrecking things. Thankfully, you hadn't spoken to them before that point, so there wasn't anything to find."

Cruz didn't bother to add the other, more gruesome, truth. If Tony had wanted to hurt the Riccis, he could've done that at any time. Instead, he'd waited to make his move while they were away, at their weekly mass.

She nodded slowly, looking slightly comforted by the awful conversation. "So he's throwing a tantrum."

Cruz smiled. "I guess that's one way to look at it. But here's the thing. The louder he yells, the easier it will be to find him."

Gina inched closer to Cruz, tucking herself against his side and pulling his arm around her shoulders. "Is this okay?"

"Yeah," Cruz answered, careful not to let his

shock register in his voice. He brushed locks of dark hair off her shoulder, letting the silky strands slide between his fingers, half-mesmerized by the heavenly feel and scent.

"What do we do now?" she asked.

It took a moment for the question to make sense in Cruz's mind, and for his wandering thoughts to return to the moment at hand.

"We stay here, safe and together, while Derek and local law enforcement keep looking for him," he said, liking the notion more by the second. "Tony can't stay off the grid much longer without making himself look suspicious. People get busy, go on trips, take a few days to be alone, but they come back. They move on with their lives. So my family will watch for signs of his return home or to his office, while I keep you out of sight."

"What happens when they locate him?" Gina asked.

"If he shows up at his home or office, a West Liberty officer will invite him to the station for questioning in your disappearance. Even if his lawyers get him out before charges can be pressed, at least we can follow him from there. Just being called out at this point should be enough to shake him."

Gina yawned.

Cruz turned his lips toward her head. "You

should probably get some sleep," he said softly. "Derek is spending the night outside your folks' place, keeping a quiet watch from several houses away. You can give them a call in the morning if they don't call you before then."

"I won't be able to sleep," she said. "And I don't want to be alone. Do you mind if I stay with you a little longer?"

His heart gave a heavy kick and he fumbled for how best to respond. Gina was soft and warm against him. Her heat registered through the material of both their shirts and seared him in wholly perfect ways. The sweet scent of her erased any need to check in with his cousins right away.

"All right," he agreed, adjusting her in his arms so her head rested against his chest. Then he let himself relax and enjoy the moment, delighted that she wanted to be there with him too, even if it was only to avoid being alone. And he wished, self-indulgently, that one day soon, he could tell her exactly how little he minded her choosing him over an empty room and bed. And how much he'd like her to choose him again every night.

Chapter Fifteen

Cruz woke to the blessed scent of fresh coffee. He'd stayed up long after Gina had fallen asleep on the couch, tucked sweetly against him as if she belonged there. He'd done some research on the Marino family, Tony and his father in particular, then talked to Derek off and on until nearly dawn, sorting his complicated thoughts on the case and keeping Derek company while he watched over the Riccis.

He hadn't dared to move Gina to her bed, fearing the trip would wake her, and knowing she needed her sleep. So he'd tipped her over where she sat, slid a pillow under her head in his absence and covered her with a blanket before sneaking away to catch a few hours of sleep for himself. He'd briefly entertained the thought of carrying her to his bed, but that seemed like a bad idea for multiple reasons, not the least of which was that every time he touched Gina a little, he longed to touch her more.

The thought of touching her more had kept him from falling asleep immediately when he'd finally crawled into bed, despite the hour. Now he was groggy and that made him cranky. So he padded on autopilot toward the scent of freshly brewed coffee, like a sailor following his siren song. He placed mental wagers on how many cups it would take to truly wake him and doubted anything could do the job after roughly three hours of sleep.

Until Gina came into view, standing near the glass deck doors again, staring at something beyond. His gaze trailed over her long dark hair, hanging in waves over her shoulders and across the crisp white cotton of her T-shirt. The reflection of her pretty face was visible in the glass, and her wide brown eyes seemed fixed on a pair of red birds in the apple tree out back.

Cruz let his greedy gaze travel down her back to the pink plaid sleep shorts and bare legs beneath. A surge of adrenaline coursed through him, doing more to wake him than any amount of caffeine ever could. And a low groan escaped his lips.

Gina spun, eyes bright and smile wide. She had a white mug clasped between her small hands.

Cruz feigned a stretch and yawn to cover

the less appropriate sound he'd made a moment before. "Good morning."

"Good morning," Gina echoed.

He headed for the coffeepot, then poured a mug to the brim. "Thanks for this," he said, turning back to her before taking a hearty sip.

Gina bit her lip. "Of course." She moved to the island then, claiming a seat on the stool across from where he stood. "Tell me when you're more awake, because I have an idea I want to run by you," she said.

He hoped idly that her idea aligned with any number of the ideas he'd fallen asleep enjoying, but assumed he wasn't that lucky. "What is it?"

"I've been avoiding social media all this time, trying to stop Tony from somehow finding me, but websites like Facebook are great resources for us too. Even if Tony hasn't updated his feed, his mom or someone else who's seen him might have." She fidgeted, then bit her lip again. "Sorry. I've been limiting my caffeine intake since finding out about the baby, but I've had two cups in the last hour, and I think I've reached my limit."

He laughed, buoyed by her smile and envious of the caffeine rush. "I'm working on catching up with you," he said, lifting his mug in evidence. "Meanwhile, keep going."

She folded her hands on the island and took

a deep breath. "What if I reach out to a few people online, only two or three, and only the ones I'm certain will be willing to help me build a case against Tony? I can make a new account and keep the exchanges private."

Cruz sucked down the rest of his coffee, scorching his tongue and burning his throat in the process, needing the caffeine to take hold before discussing anything that could wind up putting Gina in harm's way. "Care if we have breakfast while we talk this through?" he asked. He grabbed the English muffins and a jar of peanut butter from his pantry, then raised them in Gina's direction.

"Sure." She smiled. "Thanks."

Cruz set the items on the counter.

Gina left her seat and met him at his side. "Do you have an apple? I can slice one to go with the muffins."

He pointed to the fridge, and Gina retrieved an apple.

She went to work on that, while he split two muffins and dropped the pieces into his toaster.

"I like the overall concept you've got going," he said, "but I don't like the risk." He waited for her to argue. When she didn't, he went on, "You'd be putting a lot of trust in people from a very untrustworthy guy's world, in order for this to work. And that makes me nervous," he admitted. He took another sip of coffee and reminded himself to think about her proposal logically and cautiously, but not so overprotectively. He felt, belatedly, a little like Captain Obvious, since Gina knew better than most people exactly what she could be getting into.

"That's true," she agreed, "but people as awful as Tony inevitably make a few enemies along the way. They just aren't outwardly vocal about it, so we need to find them."

"I take it you have some ideas about who to contact first," he said, pouring a second mug of black coffee and trying to accurately weigh the risk against the potential reward.

"I think so," Gina said. She leaned against the counter. "I know you're worried about me, but you don't need to do that. You can oversee all the online exchanges, and if anyone is willing to meet in person, you can choose the place, come with me or go alone. I don't care, as long as the end result is Tony behind bars."

He couldn't argue with that. The plan was sensible and smart. Plus, it kept her out of harm's way. The worst thing that could happen was if one of the people she reached out to snitched to Tony. But even then, Gina would still be safe with Cruz. "Seems like you've thought it all through," he said. "I don't hate it."

"Good," she answered, dividing the apple slices between two plates with a grin.

Cruz finished his new cup of coffee, then added peanut butter to the toasted muffin halves and placed two beside the apples on each plate.

He carried their breakfasts to the small dinette near his sliding glass doors, and Gina followed. They ate companionably for several minutes before he spoke again. Stomach full and caffeine working, he had more questions. "Who do you have in mind for your targets?"

Gina leaned forward, hands folded beneath her chin. "Tony has a sister he doesn't speak to, and a secretary he treats like trash. Actually, I think he fired her a few months ago. There's also an ex-girlfriend who avoids him like he's contagious at every gala and fundraiser. She even left once, immediately after seeing us arrive."

"Let's skip the sister," Cruz said. "Families are complicated, but I like the others as potential resources." A recently fired employee and ex-girlfriend who wouldn't share the same room with Tony were compelling witnesses. Both would also have access to information

Cruz's family might potentially use to build their case.

Gina finished her apple slices with a thoughtful expression. "I was also friends with the girlfriend of Tony's friend Ben," she said. "Her name's Celia, and Ben works at Tony's company. I think Celia would help me get into contact with the secretary and old girlfriend. She might even have information on what Tony's been up to lately, if he's spoken with Ben."

Cruz stretched back in his seat, feeling more like himself by the minute. "The friend's girlfriend is unlikely to feel obligated to tell Tony you contacted her. She might tell her boyfriend, though. What's he like?"

"Nice," Gina said. "He seemed like a good guy. I could always tell when he thought Tony was being awful to me. He didn't speak up like he should've, but he also never behaved like Tony. They've been friends a long time. I sometimes got the feeling a shared history, more than actual affection, was what kept them in one another's circle."

"If Ben works at Tony's family's company, he might've also worried about losing his job," Cruz added.

Gina chewed the edge of her lip as she nodded, lost in thought once more.

Cruz longed to soothe her tortured lip, but tried not to stare.

Gina never seemed to stop thinking, planning or troubleshooting. It was no wonder she'd stayed off Tony's radar for as long as she had. She was too smart for him, and he must've hated that.

Cruz smiled at the thought.

"What?" she asked, freeing her lip and drawing his eyes up to hers.

He lifted his palms, pleading the Fifth.

Her phone rang, and she released him from her gaze. "It's my parents."

"Take it," he said. "I've got this."

Gina carried her phone to the couch, folding herself onto the cushions with a warm, anticipating smile. "Hello?"

Cruz allowed himself a moment to wonder what it might be like to keep her in his life after her danger had passed. Would she be interested in him if she no longer needed his protection? Was the attraction he felt between them born of heightened emotions alone? Did she feel it too?

He carried their plates to the sink and turned the water on. How great would it be to see her baby born? To be asked to stick around and be a part of their lives?

He shook his head and scrubbed the plates

a little harder. Clearly, the coffee hadn't given his muddled brain as much clarity as he'd thought. There wasn't any reason to think Gina would want to see him after this was over, let alone want him hanging around to watch her raise her baby.

Or be part of both their lives in a permanent way.

He finished the dishes, then wiped the counters as he thought about the plan she'd proposed over breakfast. It was a good plan.

Gina made her way back to the kitchen a few moments later, the cell phone no longer at her ear.

"How's your mama?" he asked.

"Good." Gina smiled. "They're getting new carpet, and she promised to call me every morning at this time, so we'll always have that to look forward to." Her lip quivered, whether in sadness or joy, he wasn't sure.

Cruz opened his arms to her, and she fell easily against his chest, wrapping him in a tight squeeze. "You really are a hugger," he said, tightening his grip when she tried to escape.

She laughed against his chest. "And you aren't?"

"Only for you," he admitted, and she seemed to melt against him.

"Thank you," she whispered. Her cheeks were pink when she stepped away from him.

He would've given everything he owned to know what she was thinking.

"I gave my obstetrician the number of my burner phone. I hope that's okay. You were very specific about who I could talk to on it, but I don't know how long I'll be living here, and it'll be time for me to see her again in about ten days. I didn't want to cancel the appointment if I didn't have to."

"Sounds good," he said. "I wasn't thinking about your doctor when I set up the phones. I didn't know you saw a doctor regularly. Is that normal? You're both okay?" He tried to look less clueless than he suddenly felt.

"Yeah." Gina smiled. "We're fine. Pregnant women usually see their doctors monthly until the last month or two. Then I'll see her, or someone else, more often."

He nodded, making a mental note to look into her doctor's background and office location. "I can take you to your appointments if you want. Just let me know."

"I will. Thanks."

Cruz pushed his hands into his pockets. "I guess we should see about putting your plan into motion."

"Really?" she asked, brightening at the word. "Now?"

"Sooner is probably better, right?" he asked. "For what it's worth, you should know I think you're brave for wanting to help. Knox was thrilled to get that list of people in Tony's circle last night, and I know this will help too." He grinned, feeling misplaced pride bloom in his chest. Gina wasn't his to take pride in, but he couldn't help the wave of good vibes. "You might wind up bringing Tony down all by yourself," he said, punctuating the words with a wink.

"Sure." She laughed. "Just me and my handsome bodyguard." Her gaze drifted over his chest, then up to his lips, stealing the air from his lungs in a long delicious burn.

When her eyes met his, he took a step closer, enjoying the crackle of energy around them.

The doorbell interrupted like a wet blanket on a fire, and he cursed whoever waited outside.

"Be right back," he said. His steps were light as he went to see who had the world's worst timing.

Gina had been flirting with him. She was looking at his lips, and someone had the nerve to visit? At that moment?

He swallowed a groan as he checked the porch through his front window.

Derek waved, already watching the window. "Derek's here," he announced, opening the door with a less than welcoming expression.

His cousin strode inside, casting a curious look at Cruz on his way to the kitchen. "I've been awake for twenty hours, and in a car for nine. I'm stiff, tired and sore. I need coffee and a lengthy massage."

Cruz pushed the door shut and locked it behind him. "You can have my coffee, but I'm not giving you a massage."

Derek waved a greeting to Gina as he poured, then gulped from a mug.

"What brings you by?" Cruz asked, joining them in the kitchen and hoping there was a quality reason for the interruption.

Derek took his time on the coffee, eyes closed and apparently two blinks away from dropping asleep on the floor.

"Are you okay?" Gina asked, sincere concern on her pretty brow.

His eyes peeled open, and he seemed to struggle with focus for a moment. "Yes. Tired."

She looked to Cruz.

He shrugged. "Go on," he urged. "Tell me what you know, then you can black out on the couch and I'll give Allison a call so she doesn't worry."

Derek finished the coffee, then set his empty mug on the counter. "A doorbell camera on a home at the end of the Riccis' block caught Tony's car turning onto the street around the time of the break-in. It's not a smoking gun, but considering everything else, it's going to strengthen the case. Knox is working on that now."

Gina covered her mouth, and her eyes went wide.

Cruz moved to her side, eyes trained on his partner. "That's incredible. Nice work, man."

Derek's smile widened as he stumbled clumsily toward the couch. "It gets better. Knox went out to shake some trees about an hour ago, and ran into Tony arriving at work, as if it was just another day at the office. He didn't know about the doorbell camera yet, so he invited him downtown for a chat about the missing Ricci girl." He waved at Gina as he collapsed onto the couch. "Now Knox is waiting on the Marino family attorney to arrive so Tony can be questioned."

Cruz felt Gina's eyes on him, and he turned to meet her gaze. "How do you feel about a trip to the station?"

Chapter Sixteen

Gina hurried into the room Knox indicated, then started at the sight of Tony and an older man on the television. Her heart pumped and ached as she struggled for breath. The sight of him induced a powerful need to run.

"It's okay," Cruz said. "Do you want to sit?"

Gina shook her head, at a complete loss for words and willing the ringing in her ears to subside. She crept carefully toward the screen, her muscles tense and chest tight.

Tony looked bored as Knox entered the room.

The older man beside Tony, presumably his attorney, shifted forward on his seat. "Deputy Winchester, I trust you've returned to apologize to my client and me for wasting our time."

Knox stared, blank faced. "No, sir."

"Then I hope you were able to come up with something more substantial than a list of unrelated crimes, the victims of which, excluding Gina Ricci, my client has never even heard of," he said.

Knox opened the file folder he'd carried back into the room, then fanned a set of photos onto the table.

Cruz moved to Gina's side and set his hand against her back for support.

"What's this?" The attorney dragged the images closer, then dared a look at Tony's unchanged expression.

"Those are the photos of Mr. Marino's car on the street where a break-in occurred last night." Knox took the seat across from the other men.

The attorney shoved the photos away. "Another crime? Do you plan to pin every broken law in Kentucky on my client before we leave here today? Which will be soon," he added, a note of threat in his tone. "Furthermore, what are you attempting to make of a grainy surveillance photo of a car resembling my client's Volvo, on a public street at a decent hour?" He released a dramatic labored sigh.

Tony alternated between examining his nails, smirking at Knox and glaring at the camera, never speaking a word.

"How can he be so cocky?" she whispered. She'd seen him behave this way before, superior and untouchable, but never when faced with a deputy sheriff for crimes he obviously committed. Wasn't he nervous at all? "He killed a man, brutally attacked a woman and broke into my parents' home. Still he sits there as if this is all a game. As if people don't matter, their possessions and lives don't matter." Gina wrapped her arms around her middle, terrified once more by the possibility of what he might do to her baby given the chance.

The attorney stretched upright, buttoning his suit jacket and glowering at Knox. The arrogance and condescension in his expression were thick and intimidating, even through the shared wall. "We're done here. I suggest you get your act together before approaching my client again, unless you'd like me to file harassment charges. I'll be reaching out to your superior this afternoon, so we don't have to get that far." He moved toward the door and Knox opened it. The attorney jerked his head in the direction of the hall, directing Tony to leave, then he followed Knox out.

Tony stood slowly, eyes fixed on the camera, then slunk in that direction, like the lethal predator he was.

Gina's stomach clenched and her breath caught as Tony grew larger on-screen.

He lifted a hand and wiggled his fingers while staring angrily back at her.

"Anthony," the attorney called, poking his head back through the open door.

Tony's lip curled in a feral mix of distaste and amusement. As if he knew she was there, knew she was shaking. And could see her spiraling.

As if he was going to make her pay, and she knew it.

She closed her eyes and felt Cruz shift positions. When she opened her lids, it was the protector, not the monster, looking back.

Cruz had moved into the space between her and the television. He raised his brows, then widened his stance, lowering himself by several inches, bringing his face closer to hers. "You're with me now," he said. "And Tony Marino is never getting near you again."

She released a shuddered breath as she stepped against him and pressed her cheek to his chest, the way she had earlier that day. There was so much to hope for in his words, and she needed every one of them to be true.

GINA WOKE EARLY the next morning after her worst night's sleep in weeks. Seeing Tony sneer, knowing he was close enough to punch a hole through the wall and grab her, had been more upsetting than she'd realized at the time. The effects of his stare, combined with memories of his wrath, had kept her awake long after her body and mind had begged for rest.

Then, before she'd realized she finally drifted off, the sounds and scents of breakfast had filtered images of Cruz into her mind. She'd opened her eyes to a powerful sense of relief, and smiled at her current situation. Tony couldn't hurt her anymore, but her heart would surely break when it was time to walk away from Cruz.

She'd become unreasonably attached to her new protector and friend. At first, she'd been drawn to his face and attitude, but later, as they'd talked and spent time together, she'd become even more interested in his steadfast sincerity, kind heart and sense of honor. Cruz made her laugh, and he seemed to connect with her on some unexplainable level, in ways she'd never experienced. Life with him over the last few days, despite the peripheral awfulness, had been easy and natural. It was as if they'd known one another for years instead of days. The results were peaceful and pleasant, things she didn't want to let go. And the more he told her about himself and his family, the more she wanted to learn. She hoped to meet his big family, see where he'd come from and hear stories about him as a kid.

When she thought of leaving his life, after it

was safe for her to go, she knew a piece of her heart would surely chip off and stay with him.

But for now, she'd take the moments as they came.

She and Cruz parted ways after breakfast. Gina took her mom's call, and he went to take a shower. She curled on his couch to think after saying goodbye to her folks. She still needed to reach out to Tony's friend's girlfriend, Celia. She just hadn't decided how to start the complicated conversation. It wouldn't come as a surprise to the other woman that Gina had run away. Celia had been around long enough to know Tony was controlling and temperamental. She'd heard the way he spoke to Gina when they were together. She'd seen the bruises Gina always claimed were a result of her clumsiness, rather than Tony's hands. The complicated part for Gina now was determining the right way to ask for help and possibly relevant dirt on a dangerous and powerful man.

"Yeah." Cruz's voice carried through the home as he opened the bathroom door. A grand puff of steam swept into the hallway, bringing with it heady scents of his body wash, shampoo and cologne.

Cruz strode barefoot, in jeans and a gray V-neck T-shirt, toward his living room, smiling at Gina as he pressed the phone to his ear. "I was in the shower. Can't I have ten minutes to myself?" He rolled his eyes, smiling wickedly as he approached his desk. "She's fine. Everything is fine. We're the ones just sitting around waiting for information."

Gina patted the cushion at her side, and Cruz carried his laptop with him to join her.

"Anything new on Tony?" he asked whoever was on the other end of the line.

The sound of her ex's name sent a shiver down her spine.

The look he'd given her through the police station camera returned to her like a punch. There had been something unnatural in his eyes, and she no longer worried he'd fight her for custody of their child. Now she feared neither of them would survive if he had his way.

Cruz reached for her. "You okay?" He set his phone on one leg. The screen was dark, and the call disconnected.

She forced her shoulders back and her chin up. "Yeah. Who was on the phone?"

"Derek." Cruz said the word with a chuckle. "He's tailing Tony and reporting in periodically. So far, there's nothing to report, which means he's bored and checking in to pass his time more than anything."

"Wow," she said with a disbelieving smile. "Has he even had time to go home and shower?" He'd been sound asleep on the couch when Gina and Cruz had left for the police station.

Gone when they'd returned.

"I don't know," Cruz said, "but he's still a little sleep deprived and slaphappy."

Gina gave a soft laugh. "You and your family are pretty amazing. You know that? Actually, you probably hear that a lot, but I can't stop thinking it. So, I figured it was time I said so."

He grinned. "You think I'm pretty amazing?"

"Yeah." She nodded, brows raised. "You took my case, knowing I couldn't pay you, and now I've got five Winchesters in two towns trying to fix my mess. So, absolutely. Never mind the fact that you're letting me stay here, feeding me and acting as my personal chauffeur."

"Lawmen chase bad guys," he said with a smile and a shrug. "It's their job, and I think it's in my family's DNA. I let you stay here so I can keep you close. For safety's sake." He winked, and warmth spread through her body.

"What about you and Derek?" she asked, trying to learn more about his day-to-day when she wasn't there. "Surely you have other, paying cases."

He smiled. "Nothing more pressing than capturing a dangerous stalker and protecting the innocent."

She rolled her eyes, knowing he'd stopped himself short of saying the word *victim*, and she hated being a victim.

"You looked upset a minute ago," Cruz said, catching her gaze with his, then waiting for a response. "You want to talk about it?"

"Not really." She was trapped somewhere between wanting to hash out her extremely complicated feelings for Cruz and not wanting to dwell on what couldn't be changed. She sank back against the cushions with a sigh. "I can't shake the feeling Tony knew I was there yesterday," she said instead. "The way he looked into the camera. The expression he gave. I feel as if something bad is coming," she admitted. "Like there was meaning in that dead-eyed look."

Her phone rang before Cruz could respond, and she stretched to retrieve it from the table. A spark of fear ignited instantly. She'd already spoken to her parents, and they'd agreed to talk again tomorrow. They would only call a second time if something was wrong.

She tensed as she brought the device onto her lap. An unknown number filled the screen.

Cruz frowned. "It's probably a wrong number, but why don't you answer on speaker?"

"You said not to answer unknown numbers," she said, wholly terrified to press the button, which suddenly felt like the switch for an explosive.

Cruz smiled. "I told your folks that. I'm here, and I'm keeping a list of numbers who call, especially those that aren't automated sales numbers."

Gina nodded, liking the possibility of a telemarketer more than any of the ideas circling her mind. She inhaled, then prepared to make her voice as flat and bland as she could, hoping not to sound too much like herself. "Hello?"

A dark chuckle rose through the speaker in response. "I told you I could find you anywhere," Tony said, a mix of satisfaction and victory in his husky tone. "You can't run forever, baby doll, and your days of hiding are already numbered. Keep it up, and you'll be deeply sorry."

Cruz swiped his phone to life and engaged a recording app, then circled his fingers in the air, indicating she should keep Tony talking.

Gina's mouth dried, and her tongue swelled. "What do you want?" she croaked.

"I want what's mine," he seethed, his voice dripping with venom. "I want to remind you who's in charge here. You belong to me, and I decide when you can leave. I do," he emphasized. "Me. Not you."

"I do not belong to you," she snapped. "I never did, and I will never come back. But I will make sure you pay for all the things you've done." She pressed her lips shut, feeling suddenly more angry than frightened. "That's a promise."

She braced for a cutting, threatening retort, but he only laughed. The low, maniacal sound vibrated through the phone's speaker and chilled her bones.

"You think you're so tough now," he said airily, his voice light and apparently amused. "You hide out for a couple months and think you're untouchable." He laughed again, and Gina's intuition spiked. "Baby, let me make you a promise," he said, tossing her words back at her. "You are touchable. And so is everyone you care about."

Her gaze jumped to Cruz's steady eyes. "Tony?" she asked. "How'd you get this number?"

His returning chuckle sent shards of fear into her heart. "You're not the only one who'll do whatever it takes to get their way," he said. "I'm coming for what's mine. That means you, and it includes my baby you're carrying."

Her face flashed hot and her ears began to ring. "You will never get this baby," she vowed. If she had to leave the state, the country or buy a ticket to the moon, she would do whatever it took to protect her child.

"Well." He blew out a long bored breath, as if the single word was a statement of its own. "We'll see about that," he added. "For now, you're going to have to find a new doctor."

The line went dead, and Gina threw the cell phone onto the coffee table, desperate to get away from Tony's awful threats and everything remotely connected to him.

She wanted to scream, to fight, to vomit, but she was far too shaken to do anything but try not to explode.

Beside her, Cruz tapped wildly on his phone screen, then he stopped suddenly and began to scroll. "What's your doctor's name?"

"Tulane," she said, pressing the heels of her hands against her eyes. A heartbeat later, his question clicked mentally into place. "That's how Tony got this number," she said. "I just updated my contact information with her office yesterday."

Cruz's expression fell as he pumped up the volume on his phone and turned the screen in her direction.

A local news site centered the screen. A

beautiful blond reporter stood outside Dr. Tulane's office. Bright red-lettered text scrolled along beneath her, declaring, "Breaking News" and "Local Tragedy."

"According to the Great Falls Sheriff's Department," the reporter began, "local obstetrician Melissa Tulane was stabbed outside her office early this morning when arriving for work. Sources at Falls General Hospital say the thirty-one-year-old doctor is currently in critical condition. No witnesses or details have come to light at this time, making this the third violent attack in our community this week."

Cruz lowered the phone with a curse.

Gina raised a hand to her temple, her mind and body going unexpectedly numb. "I told Dr. Tulane I was hiding from a dangerous man and she agreed to see me, off the record and pro bono, for as long as I was able to remain in town. Her name was on the stolen ultrasound photo," she said. "He used the photo to find her, and her to find my number, then he hurt her to punish me."

"This is not your fault," Cruz said, tapping the screen of his phone again. In the next heartbeat, he reached out to pull Gina near. "We need to let Knox know about the call and that Tulane is your doctor."

Gina accepted his hand, but for the first time in a long time, she didn't want comfort.

She wanted retribution.

Chapter Seventeen

An hour later, Cruz waited with Gina inside Falls General Hospital for information on Dr. Tulane's attack and current medical status. Most of the Winchesters had friends on staff willing to nose around when asked nicely. Unfortunately, none of Cruz's contacts were in the ICU today, which meant Knox had to work his magic instead. And based on how long they'd already waited for his return, Knox's magic was slow.

Gina passed the wide hallway intersection nearest the ICU, jumping each time the doors to the unit opened.

Cruz wasn't faring much better. Cell reception in the hospital was terrible, and Knox wasn't responding to his requests for updates.

To make matters worse, Derek had lost track of Tony after following him into a section of especially dense traffic near the highway headed east. Thankfully, he hadn't been anywhere near the hospital at the time of their separation, but Cruz would feel much better if he and Gina were back at his house, where she was safe and well protected, as soon as possible.

Instead, they were in the busy corridor of a massive public hospital, waiting on Knox.

Gina chewed her lip, then the edge of her thumbnail, looking paler and more on edge than he liked. She hadn't been the same since they'd learned about her doctor's attack, and it worried him. She'd wanted to apologize to her doctor, and the entire Tulane family, for her role as the unintentional link between the doctor and her attacker. He'd reiterated the obvious and known danger in that, and they'd settled on meeting Knox at the hospital, where he would deliver flowers on her behalf. Now she stood around the corner from the ICU waiting room, peeking at men and women with long faces as they ghosted in and out.

Cruz followed her gaze to the small, glass-walled space, only a few feet from the ICU doors.

"I'll bet that's her family," she whispered, eyes trained on a knot of visibly upset people.

A man holding a toddler's hand spoke with an older couple and a deputy. The gray-haired woman carried a baby, and all three adults looked as if they were on the verge of tears.

Gina adjusted her platinum wig, which seemed so incredibly obvious to him. Now that he knew her, the appearance was nearly laughable. His borrowed hoodie hung to her thighs, and the rolled-up sleeves still concealed most of her hands. She probably looked like a child in oversize clothing to everyone else at first glance. "They must be so scared right now," she said, still fixated on the family.

Cruz reached for her hand and gave a reassuring squeeze, then tugged her in his direction.

She buried her face against his chest for a long moment before pushing away once more.

"We'll figure this out," he said softly, hoping the words were true, and beginning to fear they weren't. Tony Marino had proved to be a much slipperier snake than Cruz had imagined possible.

Typically, he and Derek found their person of interest or gained the information they needed in a ridiculously short amount of time. They were a fast, sharp and effective team. An efficient tool used frequently by everyone from local law enforcement to attorneys and jaded spouses. But this case, arguably Cruz's most important one, was taking far too long to wrap up. And too many people were being hurt in the process.

"We have to stop him," Gina said. "He's completely out of control, and I'm terrified just imagining what he might do next."

"I think that's the point," Cruz said. Terror was Tony's favorite tool and the source of his power. "People in his world fear him and his family—their influence, his abuse. When you left him, you broke the pattern he counted on to maintain control, and he wasn't prepared to feel powerless. Now he's trying to draw you back to him by playing on your goodness. He's counting on you to willingly take the punishment so no one else has to."

She shuddered, then cradled her middle.

He checked his watch, then scanned the corridors in each direction. "I wish I knew what was taking Knox so long. I'm giving him another five minutes before we head out. He can call with updates."

"I'd hoped to hear about Dr. Tulane," Gina said, sounding unusually strained and appearing a little ill. "I wanted to know how she looked when he saw her."

"I know, but the fewer people who see you, the better," he reminded her gently. "As it is, Tony can ask every person in this hospital if they've seen you, and it won't matter as long as they haven't."

She released a heavy breath, then raised a hand to her forehead, where a sheen of sweat had sprouted. Red spots rose high on her cheeks, and the rest of her face appeared uncharacteristically ghostlike.

"What's wrong?" he asked more sharply than he'd intended, his usually unflappable calm completely broken by the possibility Gina wasn't well. "Are you sick? Hurt?"

"I'm pregnant," she said, attempting a joke, but not pulling it off in her current state. "Sometimes, I get woozy. It doesn't happen often anymore, but it can be intense while it lasts. I'll be fine in a few minutes."

"You need to sit," he said, sliding his arm around her back for support and guiding her toward the waiting room. "Do you need a doctor?"

At least they were already at a hospital, Cruz thought, trying to find some kind of silver lining in the new complication. He knew less than nothing about pregnant women, but he knew he needed this particular one to be okay more than he needed air.

"Actually," she said, "I might be sick. If my breakfast makes a reappearance, it has nothing to do with your cooking."

"Funny," he said, attempting to smile back as his heart rate climbed into another bracket. "What can I do for you?"

"I just need to sit a minute," she said. "Cool air and cold water always helps. I think the stress exacerbates everything, but there's not much to be done about that."

Cruz walked her into the small, window-lined waiting room, then to a set of empty chairs situated away from the family and deputy who was still chatting with them. "Here." Cruz lowered her onto an armed chair, then turned anxiously toward the small corner table with a coffeepot. "I'm going to check for water."

"Thank you." She breathed the word, then tipped forward, resting her elbows on her knees and her face in her hands.

Cruz caught the vaguely familiar deputy's eye as he approached the coffee station.

The other man's gaze slid to Gina, then back to Cruz. "She okay?"

"Shaken," Cruz said. "Otherwise, I think she'll be all right."

The knot of people he'd been speaking with drifted away, turning back to themselves for conversation.

"Any chance you've seen my brother around,

Stone?" Cruz asked, checking the name on the deputy's badge.

Stone was young and blond with a gangly appearance and general air of inexperience.

"No," he said. "I came straight here from the station when my shift began, and Knox hasn't been around."

Cruz nodded, then turned his attention to the table where a half-filled pot of coffee had gone cold. There weren't any bottles of water, but there was a stack of disposable cups.

He grabbed one, then returned to Gina.

"I'm going to find a fountain and fill this with water. I'll buy a bottle if I see a vending machine, then we're going back to my place, where you can rest. Knox can call and fill us in whenever he figures out we're gone." Cruz strode back to the deputy's side. "Keep an eye on her for a few minutes?" he asked, tipping his head to Gina. "I'm going for more water and a nurse if I can find one. If you see a medical professional of any kind before I get back, have them talk to her."

"Will do," Stone assured him, then he turned his back to Gina and crossed his arms like a long-limbed, baby-faced bodyguard.

"Thanks," Cruz said. He grabbed the empty pitcher, then moved purposefully toward the ICU.

When he saw Knox with a nurse at the end of the hall, Cruz broke into a jog.

GINA OPENED HER eyes to the sounds of subtle chaos. A soft bell registered through the hospital's PA system, followed by the announcement of a Code Blue.

Thankfully, the nausea she'd been experiencing off and on for months was slowly subsiding, and her ability to think of something other than passing out had returned. What she needed to know now was if Dr. Tulane was the patient in need.

Gina straightened in the uncomfortable chair and focused on the sounds of charging feet. A crash team ran past the small waiting room, drawing Gina upright. The people Gina had suspected were her doctor's family spilled into the hall, looking horrified and drifting toward the ICU doors as they closed behind the cluster of men and women dressed in blue scrubs, masks and gowns.

The deputy, who'd been diligently standing guard before Gina, moved to the edge of the room, and beckoned them back. "Y'all need to wait here," he instructed, garnering an array of desperate and angry looks from the adults.

Gina inched closer, wishing she could tell

them how sorry she was and knowing now wasn't the time.

A moment later, a doctor in full scrubs and mask darted out from the ICU and ushered the family through the doors, pointing in the direction the team had gone. He was dressed in blue from head to toe, like the others who'd just rushed past. He moved to the deputy next, keeping his voice low and urgent, hands gesturing toward the ICU doors.

Gina crept closer still, heart rate climbing as she tried to make sense of what was happening, and of the awful icy coil in her gut.

The deputy's expression changed, and he looked over his shoulder to Gina.

The doctor followed his gaze, then punched the deputy hard in the abdomen. When he pulled his fist away, the scalpel she hadn't noticed before was crimson with blood.

A scream caught in Gina's throat, choking off her voice and her breaths while cementing her feet to the floor.

Tony's violent gaze was suddenly unmistakable, sandwiched neatly between the protective mask and puffy hair covering. "Hello, baby doll."

"No." She forced her heavy feet to move, then darted backward, into the waiting room.

He snaked one arm out and caught her wrist

in a vise of his fingers before she could reach the coffeepot she'd planned to use as a weapon.

"No!" she screamed, finally finding her voice and employing it at maximum capacity.

Tony jerked her painfully to him and tipped the bloody scalpel toward her middle. "Say another word, or fight me, and your baby will pay."

On the floor, the deputy clutched his walkie-talkie with one hand, the other palm pressed tightly against the blooming wound in his gut.

Tony yanked her into the hallway and nearly off her feet.

Tears spilled across her cheeks as she stumbled along at his side, dragged swiftly away from the waiting room.

"Gina!" Cruz's voice echoed in the otherwise quiet hallway, his footfalls beating a steady and increasing rhythm in her direction.

She heard the rumble and bounce of a falling water bottle, and a dozen voices lifting into the air.

"Knox!" he screamed. "He's got her!"

Gina strained to see behind her, to catch sight of her hero one last time.

"Freeze!" Cruz yelled, voice frantic and fervent as he rounded the corner in her direction, closing the distance between them like a track star. He pumped his arms and knees, reaching for the sidearm that wasn't there because he'd locked it in his glove box before they'd left his Jeep. He wasn't permitted to carry it into the hospital.

Gina's heart swelled, and the fear heated to anger inside her. *No more running*, she told herself. *It's time to fight.* "No!" Her feet tangled and her ankles twisted as she grabbed Tony's hand on hers and tried to pry it loose. "Stop!" she screamed. "Help!" And instead of tripping over herself, trying to keep up with him, she dug her sneakers into the ground and forced him to drag her.

Yes, he'd threatened her baby, but whatever he could do to her now, while in a hurry and on the run, would be nothing compared to what would happen if she let him haul her away and take his time.

Tony slammed a shoulder against the stairwell door, and the barrier swung freely open.

"No!" she screamed again, this time throwing her legs out from under her and dropping onto the floor like a 150-pound sack of potatoes. She curled into the fetal position to protect her abdomen.

A string of biting cusses flew from his lips as his forward momentum halted.

He tried to pull her up by her arms, but there wasn't any time, and the cavalry was closing in. His scalpel clattered to the floor and she kicked it away.

"Great Falls Sheriff's Department," Knox bellowed, quickly catching up to his brother's side.

Gina cried out with relief as the stairwell door slammed closed and Tony disappeared behind it.

Chapter Eighteen

Cruz waited impatiently near the back of the emergency room while Gina was seen by a doctor. Her shaky voice mingled with a deeper, more sedate tenor behind a blue privacy curtain.

She'd needed the exam because Cruz had left her in the hands of someone else, and they had both failed her.

He ran through all the possible scenarios, trying to determine a better course of action. One that wouldn't have ended with her nearly abducted, and a deputy in surgery. But he kept coming up short. Maybe Cruz should've insisted the deputy fetch the water. Or called the hospital cafeteria and had water delivered. Something. Anything other than leaving her side, knowing Tony was out there somewhere, waiting to get his hands on her. Cruz had woefully underestimated his opponent's level of determination, and that mistake could've cost Gina's or her baby's life.

Now it was Deputy Stone's family gathered anxiously in a waiting room, desperate for news of his well-being.

Cruz blamed himself for that too.

If there was an upside, in addition to Gina's safety, it was that the crash team had been successful. They'd saved Dr. Tulane, likely after Tony had made a second attempt on her life. Presumably to create a satisfactory distraction and gain access to Gina.

Cruz checked his phone for the tenth time in as many minutes, eager for updates on Deputy Stone, Dr. Tulane or Gina's friend Heather, who still hadn't woken after Tony's attack. Then he double-checked for a missed text from Knox, who was yet again nowhere to be found. He'd last messaged to say he'd lost track of Tony in the stairwell, and was on his way to talk to hospital security about accessing the cameras. But he hadn't returned or texted again, and Cruz was undecided about whether or not to worry. Knox could handle himself in a fair match, even against a sociopath like Tony, but no one was on even footing if they were ambushed.

Cruz prayed his little brother hadn't been ambushed.

He turned back to the blue curtain, longing to yank it aside and know if Gina and the baby were okay. He wanted to be there for her if she was scared, or needed someone to lean on, but he'd been forced outside the flimsy barrier by protocol and manners. He wasn't family, so he wasn't entitled to know anything about her medical condition or care, and he wasn't rude enough to invite himself into the circle. She likely would've agreed for his sake, or from some misguided perception of obligation, but that wasn't the reason he ever wanted to be included.

Instead, he paced the few short steps back and forth, mentally preparing for the worst.

The curtain slid back on his second pass, and Cruz nearly jumped.

A handsome doctor ushered Gina out, a warm smile on his clean-shaven face.

Cruz felt a scowl form. He forced his attention to Gina, who looked unsteady, but less pale than she had before. "How are you?" he asked. "Is the baby okay?"

She nodded quickly, then smiled shyly as she stepped away from the doctor and wrapped her arms around Cruz's middle.

The simple move warmed him and softened the ache in his chest. She and her baby were okay, and Gina wanted his comfort. Not the smiling doctor's. His arms closed protectively, possessively, around her, and he planted a kiss against the top of her head. The move was easy and natural. So much so that it stunned him briefly.

The doctor crossed his arms and nodded smugly. "She and your baby are going to be just fine," he assured him. "Nothing a little rest and hydration won't cure. Maybe a little less excitement moving forward," he suggested. "Over-the-counter meds for pain. Long showers, foot and back rubs for tension and muscle aches. Consult with a counselor in a day or two, just to follow up after the trauma." His expression turned compassionate and deadly serious. "You might feel emotionally fine now, but these things have an uncanny way of sneaking up and taking hold if we ignore them."

Gina nodded, but didn't release Cruz or step out of his embrace.

"For now," the doctor continued, raising his gaze to meet Cruz's, "lavish them both with attention and kindness. That's my prescription for a happy relationship, and it's solid advice. I know because my wife has yet to disagree, and believe me, if I was wrong, she'd let me know."

An incredible feeling rushed through Cruz as he accepted the paperwork passed to him, then watched in stunned silence as the doctor strode away. The concept of Gina being his to care for, and him being the one responsible for lavishing her and her child with love and attention, rattled something loose inside him. And he was instantly certain there wasn't anything he wanted more.

He hadn't known her long, but he loved and appreciated what she was made of, and he saw a kindred spirit in her. She was sweet, but strong, kind and wise. Gina embodied all the things he aspired to be every day. And she loved her family. He knew his family would love her too, if she'd agree to give him a try as more than just her bodyguard, once the danger had passed.

"I'm sorry," she muttered into his shirt, still clinging to him as if he might disappear. "I shouldn't have insisted we come here. I shouldn't have been anywhere near the ICU today."

Cruz pulled back for a look at her face. "You know what I'm going to say about that, right?" He raised one brow and waited for her responding smile, all while imagining how to convince her to date again, when her most recent boyfriend was on a murderous rampage.

"Maybe," she said. "Were you thinking I'm not the boss of you, and you didn't have to listen to me when I asked to come here?"

An unexpected chuckle rose from his chest. "I'm pretty sure you actually are the boss of me," he said, noting a new reverence in his voice and wondering if she heard it too. "But none of this is your fault." He turned her in his arms and set a hand against the curve of her back. "How about we get you home for that shower, a couple pain relievers and some rest?"

She leaned against his side as they made their way back toward the emergency room exit, where they'd parked his Jeep. "The doctor said there would be pampering," she said.

Cruz's smile brightened. "I believe he said lavishing."

"That sounds spectacular," she returned casually. "He's definitely my favorite adviser now."

Cruz snorted, not bothering to hide his borderline belligerent smile. "I guess he was right. You seem like you're going to be just fine."

"Depends on how the rest of the day goes," she quipped. "I'm quite particular about my lavishing."

Cruz laughed outright, a storm of filthy thoughts pushing into his mind. "We should probably also talk about what happened," he said. "The doctor was right. It helps to talk, and trauma can sneak up on you later if you don't deal with it now. And we should follow up with him for recommendations on counselors, unless you already have one you trust."

Gina slowed, peering up into his face. "Thank you for caring enough to say any of that. I will follow up. I promise. But I really shouldn't have asked you to bring me here," she said, the playful edge in her voice long gone.

"There was no way we could've anticipated Tony would come here," he said. "Not with two towns' worth of law enforcement looking for him, and Derek tailing him in another direction at the time. When I agreed to bring you, I'd assumed the biggest risk was potentially being followed home. I had a dozen alternative routes planned to lose anyone who tried."

"He's really lost it," she said, slowing her pace to a crawl. "His eyes were wild. And I still can't believe he'd come here, knowing the authorities suspect him in all those other crimes. Then he stabbed a deputy. Tried to abduct me in public while posing as a doctor. Tony never would've done anything like that before. He was always so careful about keeping his dark side off the world's radar. It's like he's had some kind of break. I want to ask what could possibly be next, but—"

Cruz's phone rang before Gina could finish

her thought, and they froze in unison, while he looked at the screen. "Knox."

She nodded, then stepped aside, pressing her back to the wall at the edge of the emergency room's waiting area.

Cruz moved with her, clearing the way for foot traffic as he answered. "What did you find?" he asked, pressing the phone to his ear.

"Nothing good," Knox said. "You still at the hospital?"

"Yeah, we're in the emergency room waiting area now," he said, turning his attention to Gina, then lowering the phone closer to her ear. "We're getting ready to head out. Where are you?"

The cries of an approaching ambulance registered in stereo, both through the phone line and on the air outside.

Knox released a deep breath. "I'm pulling up now. Don't go anywhere."

Gina frowned, and Cruz felt the wind being pressed from his chest. His brother's voice was tight, and he'd been out of contact too long. Knox had been chasing Tony on foot, then he'd planned to visit hospital security. So, why was he outside and pulling up in his cruiser?

"What happened?" he asked as the black-and-white rolled into view outside the sliding glass doors, an ambulance hot on its bumper.

"Just…" Knox came up short. "Stay there. I'm on my way in."

Cruz and Gina watched as Knox parked his car, then ran to meet the EMTs at the back of the ambulance.

Gina reached for Cruz, one hand on his arm, the other over her mouth. "Do you think it's Tony?"

"I don't know," Cruz said, knowing in his gut it couldn't be her assailant. If Knox had caught Tony, he would've led with that, but he hadn't. And the names of people Gina cared for tore through his mind like stock cars.

The gurney appeared a moment later, piloted by a pair of EMTs, an IV bag hanging high above the patient's head. A man's head, it seemed, one with dark hair.

Selfishly, Cruz hoped it wasn't someone he cared about, and the possibility Tony had changed his MO momentarily stole his breath. Derek? Blaze or Lucas?

The parade sped past them, drawing every prying eye in the waiting room, and the sight stole Cruz's breath.

The patient's face was nearly unrecognizable, unnaturally swollen and distended from a severe beating, like a boxer who'd gone ten too many rounds. And it wasn't one of Cruz's cousins.

It was Rex, Cruz's friend and informant.

Knox came to a stop as the gurney and its team raced away. "I left the hospital as soon as I got the call," he said. "I thought Rex fit the victim's description, but I wanted to be sure before I told you. When I got there, the EMTs had stabilized him and were loading him for transport. I chaperoned." He lifted, then dropped a hand, looking as helpless as Cruz felt.

"What happened?" Gina asked, forming the words he couldn't. "And when? Tony was here until you chased him away, and he was busy attacking Dr. Tulane this morning."

Cruz braced himself against the wall, mentally tracking the timeline with her and waiting for Knox to speak.

Knox set his fluttering hands on his hips, then pinned Cruz with a determined look, before the words began to flow. "The EMTs think he was likely attacked late last night, based on bruising and the condition of the wound." He stopped short, Adam's apple bobbing. "His assailant left a note, stabbed through his palm with a hunting knife. The medics think he's probably been out cold since then. He's suffered severe blunt force head trauma and lost a lot of blood."

Gina made a small strangled sound.

Cruz forced himself to stand tall, chin up and shoulders squared. It was time to fight for his friend, who couldn't fight for himself. "What did the note say?"

Knox's gaze slid from his brother to Gina, then back. "'How many more people have to get hurt?'"

Chapter Nineteen

Cruz carried a mug of hot tea to where Gina had curled onto his couch. Rex hadn't woken. Neither had Dr. Tulane or Heather. Deputy Stone was awake, but there hadn't been any updates, aside from confirmation of a successful surgery. "I hope you like chamomile," he said. "My aunt brought it here last winter when I caught a cold."

Gina accepted the mug with a soft smile. "It's great. Thank you." Her skin was flushed from a hot shower, and her eyes were bright with the effects of a much-needed nap. Now she was in her pajamas and looking ridiculously cuddly.

"I keep trying to put this day behind me," she said. "But I can't stop dwelling on all of it. I feel so awful for Tony's victims, and I'm terrified by how quickly the number is growing." She inhaled the sweet tendrils of steam

from her mug and lifted big dark eyes to Cruz.
"I hate it."

"I know." He took a seat, then pulled her feet
onto his legs. "This okay?"

She gave a small smile. "Yeah."

Cruz set his palms on her calves and his
phone on the cushion beside him. "Knox will
call as soon as he learns something new. Until
then, we hide out and save our energy. What
do you think?"

"Agreed." She sipped her tea, eyes closing
for a beat with each small swallow. "I'm really
sorry about Rex."

"Me too." Cruz ran a palm absently over the
warm skin of her leg, just above a fuzzy pink
sock and miles below her plaid cotton sleep
shorts. He'd been trying intensely not to think
about the sleep shorts. "Rex wanted to help. He
came to me, not the other way around, and he
went into this understanding the situation. If
I'd have tried to stop him, or told him it was
too dangerous, he would've told me where to
stuff that. I have faith he'll come out of this
okay, and when he does, he'll testify against
Tony."

Gina took another sip of tea. A frown formed
between her dark brows, and Cruz knew she
was worrying again.

He dragged his hands down to her socks,

getting far too distracted by the feel of her skin beneath his palms. The doctor had recommended foot rubs, and that seemed a safer activity for his wandering mind than caressing her calves. "I think it might be time for us to relocate," Cruz said. He pressed the pads of his thumbs against the soles of her fuzzy-socked feet, and she moaned in response.

He froze. Maybe a foot rub wasn't a great idea. Not if that was how she planned to respond.

"Sorry," she apologized. "That just felt really good, and I wasn't prepared."

Cruz grinned, enjoying the fact that he could bring her enough pleasure to make her moan. He instantly wanted to do it again. "Tony knows about me now," he said. "He saw me at the hospital and heard me calling your name. That couldn't have made him happy. All it takes is a look at the county auditor's website to find my address after he learns my name. Then he'll be on my doorstep. So, how do you feel about spending some time at my family's cabin?"

She frowned again. "I think we should do whatever you think is best. I'm out of my depth, and I trust you."

Her trust was a welcome prize. One he wasn't sure he'd earned, but was incredibly thankful to have. "I hoped you'd say that, because Derek will be calling soon to help me make the arrangements. We can leave in the morning. There should be news from Knox or the hospital by then."

She moaned again as his thumbs worked against the arches and balls of her feet. "Do you regret taking this case yet?" she asked.

"No." His grin widened as her head tipped against the couch.

Their eyes met a moment later, and he stilled, captivated by the unexpected intensity of her gaze. The heat he felt so often in her presence blazed back to life. "I saw you before you walked into my office that day," Cruz said, feeling the urge to tell her exactly how quickly he'd wanted to know her. "I hadn't seen you before, but when I did, I willed you to come inside. My cousins thought I'd lost it."

"What?" She laughed. "You saw me?"

He nodded. "I wanted to meet you the minute you came into view. If you hadn't come inside, I might've gone out to chase you down and ask your name."

Her lips parted, and her expression changed from something like wonder to a hint of disappointment. "You have a thing for blondes."

He laughed. "I love brunettes," he said. "I thought the only thing that would keep me from losing my mind completely was the fact that you were a blonde."

Her eyes twinkled with pleasure, and she set her tea aside. "Is that right?"

"Absolutely. I thought you should know."

She smiled sweetly, her full lips pressed into a tight little grin. "You thought I was pretty."

"I think you're beautiful," he corrected. "I'm glad I've gotten to know you, and I want you to know you're doing an incredible job of holding things together. In case you ever start to doubt that, don't."

Her expression softened, and she set her hand on his arm.

"The clock is ticking for Tony. His recent crime spree is evidence he's losing control. He's taking bigger chances and acting more frequently. It's only a matter of time before he's caught. All we have to do is keep you out of his hands until he's arrested. Then you'll be free to make any kind of life for yourself and your baby that you want."

"Thank you," she said. "Your continued confidence gives me hope, which is exactly what I need right now." Gina wet her lips, then lifted her gaze to meet his. "While we're making confessions and speaking truths," she began, and Cruz pulled in a slow breath, "I haven't told you how incredibly patient you've been.

With me, and with all this…mess." Her hands fluttered helplessly between them, as if, possibly, to indicate the whole reason they'd met and were hiding out together. "I don't know anyone else who would've opened their home to me the way you have. More than that, you've been a friend to me. Now you're taking care of me. Telling me to rest and bringing me tea." She shook her head. "I don't think you have any idea how much that means."

She pulled her feet away from him and sat up, tucking them beneath her.

Cruz turned, the warm vanilla scent of her shampoo pulling him a little closer. He ached to say more than he could about exactly how much he liked taking care of her, but it wasn't the right time.

"I just want you to know you've become very important to me," she said.

He searched her eyes, as if there might be more hidden there. Something she wasn't ready to say. Could she mean what he hoped she did?

"I had a good life before Tony," she said. "I was raised right, and I never got into trouble. I'd always been the shy girl no one noticed, especially not rich, handsome men." She gave a dark, self-deprecating laugh. "I was incredibly naive, but I also hadn't had any real experience with life or men. I was too trusting.

And I liked the attention so much that I let a lot of his initial offenses slide. Then, one day, the things between us weren't little anymore, and I was trapped in a nightmare. Ashamed. Embarrassed. And scared."

Cruz reached for her hand, knowing how much this confession meant to her, and wanting her to understand she could trust him with it.

She turned her palm against his, linking their fingers. Then she forced a tight smile. "I thought you should know how I wound up in this situation. I owe you that much. It's kind of my biggest life failure. My baby is the only good thing that came from any of it. Maybe that makes it all worthwhile." She shrugged. "Either way, you need to know who you're dealing with." Her cheeks reddened, and she struggled to keep her eyes on his. "Pretty girls aren't always the smartest."

"You are," he said, courage rising in his chest. If she was brave enough to share her story, maybe it was time he shared his as well.

He bit the insides of his cheeks, testing his thoughts and emotional standing. Cruz didn't tell his story often, or without significant cause, but in the name of equality and transparency, it seemed like a right and fair exchange. Gina should know he wouldn't hold back with her. He wasn't hiding a monster or anything other than a lifetime of experiences he tried daily to learn from so he could do better.

"My dad was awful to my mama." He let the words sit between them a moment before going on. "He left years before she got cancer, but while he was with us, he was terrible. He treated her like she was worthless, like she had no value, and it broke her heart. Knox and I were young, but we saw what his words did to her, saw her flinch at the put-downs that never seemed to end. He didn't always come home at night, and she'd sit up and worry. We never had enough money, but he'd blame that on her spending." He shook his head, fighting the unbearable pain in his chest. "One day he hit her. I was in middle school, but nearly as tall as him at the time, and I came for him with my bat." Cruz's jaw locked against the rage and embarrassment he knew were misplaced and pointless. "I didn't hit him, but I wanted to. Mama told me to walk away. I didn't do that either. I told him to get out. He came back the next day for his things, but we never saw him again after that."

"Cruz," Gina whispered. "I'm so sorry. I wish that hadn't happened."

"Knox and I got jobs," he said. "Eventually,

so did Mama. I thought she blamed me for a long time because money was a lot tighter without him, especially when she got sick, but she always blamed herself for keeping him around so long." He shook his head, pressing the grief and remorse aside. "I vowed as a small child that I would never intentionally belittle, degrade or devalue someone. I would never be a bully or make someone else cry so I could feel powerful. I've built my life trying to be a better man than the one who raised me. Your case hits home for me in a lot of ways, and you should know that."

The sadness in her eyes stole the wind from his lungs.

"I wish you weren't going through these things," he added, desperation gripping his heart and mind.

"At least I'm not alone anymore," she said. "It's a lot less scary with you here."

The word *scary* brought an awful image into Cruz's mind. "When I saw him with you today," he said, trailing off and struggling for words. "I haven't been that afraid in a long time."

"Really?" she asked. "Because as soon as I saw you, my fear faded, and I felt braver than I ever have."

Her sweet words unwound his remaining

tethers, and he leaned carefully in her direction, cocking a knee on the cushion between them and searching her with his gaze.

"Cruz?" she asked, her voice going husky as she glided one hand up his arm, then hooked her fingers over his shoulder. "Is this okay?" She smiled, teasing him with the words he always offered her when they touched.

"Yes," he said, setting his free hand on the curve of her waist. "Are you feeling all right?"

"I feel very well, thank you," she said. "And incredibly safe in your arms." She threaded her fingers into the hair at the back of his head and nudged him gently closer. "But I can't stop wondering how you would feel in my arms." Her sweet breath warmed his face, and his reasons for holding back became as fuzzy as his head.

He closed the remaining space between them and pressed his lips to hers.

The profound perfection of the simple act made him moan with pleasure. He drew her onto his lap, holding her close and gliding his palms against her spine. Their mouths moved together, and like everything else they'd done together, kissing Gina felt as natural as if they'd done it a thousand times.

Cruz's ringing phone forced him out of the delicious, dizzying haze. He stopped to admire

her beautiful face before answering the call.
Her flushed cheeks and swollen mouth begged
him to come back, but if this thing between
them could really be everything he wanted it to
be, then they didn't need to hurry. Right now,
he needed to take Derek's call and make plans
to get Gina safely out of town.

Chapter Twenty

"Winchester," Cruz answered, accepting the call quickly, already in a hurry to get back to Gina.

She'd slid off his lap when he took the call, and his arms ached to hold her again.

She pulled her knees to her chest and wrapped her arms around them, setting her chin on top. The shy little smile on her lips provoked another moan from him.

"Cruz?" Derek asked, a fleck of humor in his tone. "Am I interrupting something?"

"No." He grinned. "What's going on? Any news?"

Derek paused, probably hearing the entire untold story in Cruz's tone. Working with a family member he'd also grown up with, and who was a private investigator, made privacy an ongoing challenge, but Cruz wasn't talking. For now, his cousin would have to guess and infer.

He supposed he should feel guilt for shamelessly coveting, then kissing, a client, but he couldn't bring himself to manage it. Now that the line had been crossed, there wasn't any going back, for him anyway. He leaned forward and kissed her forehead, earning another smile.

"I have a little news," Derek said, "but I think your news is better. I'd sure like to hear that, or should I guess?"

Cruz smiled again. Yep. Derek heard everything, even the things folks didn't say. "You first," Cruz said, having no intention to share his news. Because they definitely needed to talk about those kisses.

"I've been sitting outside Tony's home all afternoon, waiting for a sign of him I could report to Knox, so he could come over and arrest him. No one has any idea where Tony went when he left the hospital. His car is here, but there hasn't been any movement inside. No one has come in or gone out. Security lighting came on at dusk. That's it. He had a mask on in all the hospital surveillance footage, and the images of his face are unclear."

"His car was there when you got there?" Cruz asked, his attention fixing on the conversation.

"Yeah. Officers came by and knocked. No

answer," Derek said. "Maybe he didn't take his car to the hospital. That would make more sense than giving authorities another way to place him at the crime scene. Not that Knox was able to use that very well before, when his car was on the Riccis' street at the time of their break-in."

"How'd he get to the hospital without his car?" Cruz asked. "It's not the kind of thing he'd call an Uber for. He was taking Gina somewhere. There must've been a getaway plan."

"My questions exactly," Derek agreed. "Normally, I'd say we should look for accomplices, but we know this is personal."

"Does Tony have another vehicle registered in his name?" Cruz asked.

"Nothing the Department of Motor Vehicles is reporting," Derek said.

Cruz turned to Gina for advice. "Can you think of a vehicle that isn't in Tony's name that he might have access to?" He pressed the speaker button on his phone to include Derek in the conversation with her.

She chewed her lip, eyes sliding up and to the left, searching his ceiling for an answer. When her gaze returned to his, she frowned. "He might've used one of the company SUVs," she said. "They're all identical, black with tinted windows. The company logo is just a big magnet stuck to the side when sales reps go out on business. His dad uses the fleet, without the logos, to arrive at major social events. Put three or more of them in the row, and it gets people talking, like a celebrity is arriving."

Cruz lifted his brows. Dark nondescript vehicles sounded like exactly the kind of ride an undercover killer would love to have access to. "Derek?"

"Already on it," he said. "I'll talk to Knox and see if he can get me plate numbers on the company fleet. Then I'll see if we can place one near the hospital earlier today or in the vicinity of Rex's attack last night."

"Or the doctor's office," Cruz added.

"Will do," Derek said. "Meanwhile, you'd better get packed up and ready to move. I wouldn't put that off until morning. We don't know where this guy is right now, but we know he's mad and motivated."

"Yep." Cruz disconnected the call, and smiled warmly at Gina. "How do you feel about getting on the road tonight?"

She released her knees, then pushed onto her feet. "I'll pack my things."

"Hey," Cruz said, grabbing her hand as she moved to walk away. "We should talk about that kiss before we go. Being alone in the mountains a few days could get awkward otherwise."

Gina's cheeks darkened. She squeezed his hand and locked wide eyes on his. "The kiss was nice," she said. "Doing it again seems like a great way to pass our time alone on a mountain."

Then she flashed him a smile, and headed to her room.

GINA CLOSED HER bedroom door gently, then climbed onto her bed to process. She'd kissed Cruz Winchester, and it had been even hotter than she'd imagined. Which said a lot because she had an excellent imagination.

She plucked the fabric of her shirt away from her overheated skin. Just recalling his touch sent a wave of heat throughout her body. She hadn't been kissed by many men, but her previous experiences had all been somewhat the same, and wholly unremarkable. As a result, she'd never understood other women's fascination with the act, but now she knew. And she wished she didn't have to make time for anything else ever again.

The rumble of his low tenor vibrated outside her door, and she imagined him on his way to his room to pack. Daydreams would have to wait. For now, it was time to clear out and hole up someplace out of town.

She sent out a barrage of silent prayers for the people Tony had hurt, and for those who were on his list now, as she hurriedly packed her things. A year ago, it would've taken hours, maybe days, to decide what to wear or bring. Now she could pack all her earthly possessions into two duffel bags with practiced assurance in under ten minutes. If needed, she could walk out the door with only her purse and never come back. Funny how fear had streamlined her priorities.

When she reemerged from her bedroom, Cruz was in the living room, stacking bags and lidded plastic totes near the front door. His cell phone was pressed to his ear.

"We're headed out now," he told whoever was on the line. "Within the next hour." He smiled when he saw her, then reached for her and winked.

She added her bags to the accumulating pile, then stilled to accept his soft kiss. Goose bumps rose on her arms as he smiled against her mouth, then dropped back into his conversation without missing a beat.

"Ready?" he asked a moment later, sliding the phone back into his pocket.

She nodded, and they were on their way.

The long country road rolled out before them as she dialed the number for the phone Cruz had given her parents.

Her mama answered on the first ring. "Baby? Is everything okay?"

"I'm fine, Mama," she said, smiling despite the circumstances and endlessly thankful for the gift Cruz had given her. She'd missed her folks so much while she'd been on the run. "Cruz is taking me someplace safe while his family hunts for Tony," she said. "I can't tell you much, because it's safer for us both if you don't have details. Just know that I'm safe, and happy, and this is a strategic piece of a careful plan. It won't be long before I can spend all day squeezing you and Dad and eating your manicotti by the pound."

Her mama laughed nervously. "I will make manicotti every night for the rest of my life if that's what you want. Just come home safely."

"I will," she promised. "I'm in good hands."

Cruz seemed to sit taller beside her, a growing grin on his handsome face.

She only hoped he'd still be happy with her when she was nine months pregnant and roughly the size of a barn. "I've got to go," she said. "I wanted you to know I'm okay, just in case the reception is spotty where I'm going. Cruz's family will reach out to you if they need to. Until then, no news is good news, okay?" Gina said her goodbyes, then dropped the phone into an empty cupholder in the console, fighting the sting of rogue tears.

Cruz reached for her hand, then lifted it to his lips. "You okay?" he asked, pressing a kiss against her knuckles.

"I will be," she said, and she hoped that was true.

Above them an inky sky twinkled with the light of a billion stars, and not a single other vehicle shared their road. Fields and forests lined the winding county route, and peace seemed thick upon the earth, if not yet in her heart.

They'd passed the third city limits sign when Derek's name appeared on the Jeep's dashboard display screen.

Cruz answered the call, using a button on his steering wheel. "Hey, we're about an hour outside town now. Hoping to reach the cabin in another ten. What've you got?"

"Update time," Derek said. "Nothing on Tony just yet, but a nurse in Rex's ward just reached out. She says he's awake and speaking with a deputy. She listened. Rex said Tony thought he was a cop and demanded a location on Gina. When he wouldn't give you or her up, Tony railed on him. He doesn't even remember being stabbed through the hand. Knox is on his way to Falls General now."

Cruz's jaw tightened, but relief washed over his face. "What do the doctors say?" he asked.

"According to the nurse, Rex's healing well and anticipated to make a complete recovery," Derek said. "No lasting trauma from the head injuries, and the knife didn't do any permanent damage."

Gina set her hand on Cruz's leg and offered an encouraging squeeze. Rex was going to be okay. That was the best news they'd gotten from the hospital so far. And she could only hope there would be similar calls about Dr. Tulane, Heather and Deputy Stone soon as well.

Cruz disconnected, then shot her a conflicted expression. "Knox will protect Rex while he heals. He'll build a solid case while we lie low. Meanwhile, all we have to do is stay off the grid and out of Tony's reach."

She nodded, mind racing with hope. If Rex was awake and able to testify, the case against Tony would firm up. She'd spoken to Tony on Heather's phone and again at the hospital. Rex could identify him, and soon, Dr. Tulane and Heather would too. Cruz was right when he said the clock was ticking. It wouldn't be long before Tony was behind bars, and the relief that came with that knowledge was unequivocal.

Gina just hoped Tony didn't realize how close he was to being caught, because she wasn't sure what he would be capable of if he had nothing left to lose.

"Well," she said, forcing her mind back to more-positive thoughts, "we already have a plan in motion, so our job should be easy enough." All they had to do was stay away and let the lawmen work.

Her burner phone rang, and she freed it from the cupholder. "It's my parents," she said, surprised to see their number on her screen again so soon. A bite of terror pinched her chest as she answered. "Hello?"

"Gina!" her mom yelled.

Panic seized Gina's chest. She pressed the speaker button instinctively, then moved the phone between her and Cruz. "I'm here, Mama. What's wrong?"

"She's gone," her mom cried. "No one can find her. No one can reach her. I don't know what to do." Her mama's words broke into sobs, while fear tightened around Gina's neck like a noose.

"Who's gone?" she asked, knowing the answer, but needing to hear it stated plainly before she truly lost her mind as well. "Who can't be found?"

"Your sister."

Chapter Twenty-One

Gina sat with her parents at a conference table inside the West Liberty police station. Cruz's brothers had transformed the space into a war room for finding Kayla, complete with a coffeepot, heavy stack of files and a crime board like the ones she normally saw on movies and prime-time television shows.

Her mother trembled continually from misplaced adrenaline and the threat of shock.

Her father paced the floor.

Gina held her mom's hand and tried to pay attention to the Winchesters' conversations through ringing ears. Lucas, the special victims detective who'd helped coordinate Gina's recent meeting with Kayla, had finally returned from her campus, and she didn't want to miss any details.

The men stood on the opposite side of the table, nearest the crime board featuring Tony's face and an open door. They nodded and traded information as it became available, by phone call or text, occasionally delivered in person by a uniformed officer.

Bottom line—Kayla had been missing for hours, and this too was, at least peripherally, because of Gina. It might not have been Gina's fault, but it had been because she loved her sister. And Tony had told her he could get to everyone she cared about.

Lucas turned to Gina and her folks, then took a seat with an open file, tapping a hand on the tabletop. "We know Kayla called campus security from an emergency phone following a study session with friends," he said, apparently starting from the beginning.

This was information they'd been given upon arrival. Kayla had texted her friends, saying she felt as if she was being followed, but didn't see anyone. The friends had encouraged her to use one of the campus security phones to request an escort.

"A unit responded to her call within two minutes," Lucas said, continuing his story. Kayla hadn't been there when the officer arrived. The phone had been found hanging. "A can of pepper spray was located on the ground nearby," he added.

Gina's dad made a soft choking sound, then

turned his back to the group, rubbing both palms over his face.

Her mama stared catatonically, and Cruz offered a thin utilitarian blanket to help with her shivers. When she didn't blink or acknowledge the offering, Gina helped spread the rough material over her legs, and tucked it in along her sides.

Lucas waited for her to finish before moving on. "A team of campus security agents was dispatched to canvass the area and interview students while I was en route to follow up. I spoke with a female living on the second floor of the nearest dormitory, who claims to have seen a large black SUV with tinted glass parked outside when she arrived home. That would've been only a few minutes before Kayla placed her call for an escort. A camera at that location confirmed the presence of the vehicle, and we were able to use additional surveillance footage to track it as it left campus. There wasn't, however, a good image of the driver, passenger or plate."

Blaze moved to his brother's side, coffee in one hand, a deep frown on his face. "Derek is back on reconnaissance duty. He's stationed outside the family home, keeping tabs on the Marinos. At this point, it's going to take more than a good lawyer to distance Tony from his crimes."

Lucas steepled his fingers, elbows anchored on the table. "We've established the family will cover for him, so I've sent officers to question the parents on how they plan to respond to Tony's unraveling. Hopefully, that will spur them into action. If they're hiding him and try to move him, Derek will notify us and follow."

Gina shivered, her stomach tipping and tightening with fear and nausea. She dug her phone from her bag and accessed the internet, then sent a hasty message to Celia. Gina had planned to wait until she'd arrived at the cabin with Cruz, then toil over the exact wording of her request, but time was of the essence, and she no longer cared about finesse. She tapped her thumbs against the screen, providing a rundown of events and asking Celia for any information she had or could get. Then Gina clutched the phone in her hands and waited.

"We're attempting to get a warrant for GPS information on the fleet of Marino company vehicles," Lucas said. "That will tell us everywhere each SUV has been, as well as where they are now. The family's lawyers are doing their best to slow the process, but I feel confident the judge will see our side."

Gina's dad swore, then turned back to face the room with a look of complete desperation.

"Daddy," she whispered, reaching in his direction. "Please. Sit with Mama and me."

He stared, red-faced, either unwilling or unable to move in her direction.

Her heart ached profoundly at the sight of him. Whatever pain Gina felt, knowing her sister was gone, she couldn't imagine what her parents were going through. She'd only been pregnant a few months, and would already do or give anything to protect her child. "Daddy," Gina repeated softly, turning her palm upward and curing her fingers. "Mama needs you."

A tear rolled over her father's cheek as he returned to her mother's side.

Gina mouthed the words, "Thank you," when her mother turned and pressed her cheek to his chest.

His arms went around his wife, and Gina fixed her attention on the Winchesters, hoping they were enough to stop a madman from hurting her little sister.

"What else?" Cruz asked, paging through a file of loose paperwork in his hands. "Tell me there's enough evidence to make a strong case once we get him."

"There is," Lucas said, a small flash of pleasure in his eyes. "Knox was able to identify the knife left in Rex's hand as a brand sold exclusively through the Marino family's outdoor outfitter stores. And it's an exact match for Dr. Tulane's wounds."

Cruz's lips twitched with a flicker of pride and satisfaction. "Good."

"Also," Lucas said, tapping the screen of his phone, "we pulled this image of Tony and his dad on a hunting trip about three months ago off the internet." He turned the screen to face Cruz. "The knife in this picture matches the one in evidence. Add that to the fact that Rex was able to identify Tony as the one who hired, then attacked him, and Gina can name him as her assailant, the case is getting tighter by the minute."

Blaze shifted, widening his stance and shoving his hands into his back pockets. "We've got witnesses confirming Tony's vehicle was in Great Falls on the night the building manager was murdered. A local café worker identified him as well. She said he was handing out missing persons posters of you." His gaze met Gina's and she sucked in a ragged breath.

"I was there," she whispered, the memory returning full force. "I'd given the barista a fake name out of habit. Then I saw him, and I ran." A punch of relief mixed with fear. There were so many witnesses and a load of evidence to prove Tony's crimes. When he went before a judge and jury, there would be more than just her word against his and his family's.

Eventually, the flow of information slowed to a drip, and Gina's parents went home to monitor their landline, in case Tony reached out that way.

Gina folded her arms on the conference table and set her head on top.

The police department was quiet around them. Only a handful of detectives remained, occasionally whisking past the open conference room door.

She woke to the gentle weight of Cruz's hand on her shoulder.

"Breakfast?" he said.

She didn't remember falling asleep, but the scents of fast-food hash browns and croissant sandwiches pulled her eyelids open and caused her stomach to jump with glee. She started to ask for coffee, but Cruz had already set a steaming cup before her, beside a bottle of water, and she longed to hug him for his thoughtfulness.

Lucas yawned and stretched, tired eyes hooked on Cruz. "It's been a long night. If you're not up for a drive to the cabin right now, you can always stay with Mom and Dad, you know. Or at Derek's house. He's got plenty of room, and that place is like Fort Knox."

"I think we'd better stick to the plan," Cruz answered, raising a steamy mug of coffee to his lips.

Gina's phone buzzed, and she pulled it from her pocket, half expecting to find her parents' number on the screen. Instead, she realized it was her personal phone, the burner she'd bought, not the one Cruz had given her, making the noise. And the message was from Celia.

Cruz's expression turned curious, and he moved to stand behind her, reading the screen over her shoulder.

"It's the woman I told you about," Gina explained. "Tony's friend's girlfriend. I reached out to her last night. I didn't want to put it off any longer, and Kayla can't wait."

He grunted. "You used your personal account? Your phone?"

Gina nodded. "The phone's a burner, but yes to using my Facebook account to reach out. Is that okay?"

"Maybe," he said, not sounding as certain as she'd like.

Gina read Celia's message silently, and with quick, hungry eyes.

Oh, my goodness. Are you okay? I've been worried sick about you since you disappeared. I told Ben it was probably Tony's fault. He told me to stay out of it, but I could tell things between you two weren't right. Tony showed up at Ben's house two nights ago, wanting an alibi for something he did earlier this week. He wouldn't say what it was, and when Ben didn't agree right away he threatened him with a gun! Ben agreed so Tony would leave, but he didn't want to do it. I don't understand what's going on. And Tony says you're pregnant?! Is that true? What can I do to help you? Are you somewhere safe? I can pick you up. Find you a place to stay. Maybe a hotel room under an alias?

Cruz moved to face Gina, leaning his backside against the table before her. "This is good. We can work with that. Let her know you're safe, and she should keep this conversation quiet. Don't tell her more than you have to."

Lucas lifted his chin in Cruz's direction. "What's going on?" he asked.

Cruz took a step in his cousin's direction, then turned back. "Ask if she can think of where he might be now, or if her boyfriend can think of someplace Tony would go to disappear."

Gina nodded and her thumbs flew across the screen, energized by the possibility of an inside scoop. She sent a series of short messages in response.

I'm safe. At PD now. Leaving town soon.

Ideas where Tony could've taken Kayla?

Ask Ben?

Celia's response came immediately and was equally brief.

I'm on my way to his place now. I'll ask as soon as I get there.

Gina tucked her phone away, then forced herself to sit and wait.

Nearly an hour later, Celia hadn't responded, and Cruz was visibly on edge.

Blaze rubbed his eyes, looking as exhausted as she felt. "Take my truck," he said, tossing Cruz a set of keys. "If this guy's onto you, he'll be looking for the Jeep. I'll drive that until he's caught."

Cruz snagged the offered keys from the air, then passed the Jeep's keys to his cousin.

"Thanks." He glanced at the wall clock, then Gina.

Blaze waved a hand in goodbye as he headed for the hallway. Lucas stayed tight on his heels and tugged the door shut behind them.

Cruz looked at Gina. "Hey," he said. "I know you want to stick around in case there's word on your sister, but the smart move is to get you out of town. Remove you from the game. At the very least, it could buy us some time. Meanwhile, Tony's face is going up on news media across the state, thanks to Rex's ability to identify him. There's nothing more for us to do here. And I'm willing to bet your folks will be glad to know you're out of Tony's reach. You still have your phone if you need it."

Gina's heart plummeted at the thought of leaving town with her sister missing, but Cruz and his family knew what they were doing, and she didn't want to make anything more complicated than it already was. "Okay."

She stretched to her feet, then pulled her personal phone from her pocket. No new messages from Celia. "I should probably leave this with Blaze and Lucas," she said, passing the device to Cruz. "If Celia responds, they can get the message without needing me as the middleman."

Cruz pulled her to his chest and kissed her forehead. "Good idea."

They delivered her phone to Lucas before heading into the bright sunny day.

The streets outside the sheriff's department were dense with traffic and morning commuters.

Cruz lifted his hand, and the lights of a black pickup truck flashed at them. "Blaze loves his big truck," he mused.

Gina smiled at the row of floodlights on top and massive silver grille in the front. "This is a serious ride."

"For a very serious man," Cruz agreed wryly. "Why don't you climb in while I move our things from the Jeep to this behemoth."

"Deal."

He helped Gina climb inside the too tall truck, then smiled at her for one long beat.

"Winchester!" a voice called, turning them back toward the sheriff's department. A uniformed deputy waved a hand overhead, shielding the sun with one hand and beckoning them back with the other. "Your cousin's packing up the rest of this food for the road."

Cruz smiled, obviously thankful for the offer, and likely as relieved as she was that there wasn't more bad news. He swung a questioning gaze to Gina.

She shrugged. "I'm okay. And I could eat." She hadn't taken the time to eat inside, and she regretted it sorely.

Cruz handed her the truck keys, then locked the doors before closing her in the cab and jogging back to the building.

Gina considered sliding behind the wheel. It would be impossible to feel threatened at the helm of Blaze's massive pickup.

A familiar black SUV rolled to a stop at the curb, just outside the police department parking lot, and she froze, telling herself that even Tony wouldn't come for her there.

The back passenger window powered down as she stared, and Kayla came into view. Her dark hair was tangled around a slack face, and thick silver tape ran the width of her mouth.

Gina's heart jerked into a sprint, and her eyes jumped to the building where Cruz had just gone inside.

She fumbled for her phone to text Cruz, but the other vehicle's front passenger window went down too, and Tony became visible behind the wheel. He had a handgun pointed over his seat at her sister.

Gina hastily fumbled for the door while sending the shortest text of her life to Cruz.

911

Then she moved in the SUV's direction, knowing it was her that Tony really wanted, and hoping he would let Kayla go in trade.

Tony's reptilian smile spread across his face as the rear window powered up, removing Kayla from her sight. "Where's your phone?" he called, moving the gun in a circle to indicate she should pick up the pace.

She raised the device into view, and Tony's smile became a sneer.

"Drop the phone and get in," he said. "Now!"

Her heart fell in defeat as she reached for the door. She wouldn't trade Kayla's life for her own, so she did the only thing she could.

And got in.

Chapter Twenty-Two

Gina fastened her seat belt, then twisted for a look behind her.

Kayla's head rocked on the cushioned headrest, her expression flat.

"What did you do to her?" Gina asked, turning quickly back to keep an eye on her captor, his gun and the road.

"I gave her a choice," he said. "She chose the sleeping pills I swiped from the hospital instead of my more proven method of lights out."

Gina bit her tongue against the urge to lash out. That never ended well for her, and she had her sister and baby to protect this time. Instead, she fixed her gaze through the side window and tried to track their route. "Where are we going?"

Tony checked his rearview mirror, then cut across three lanes of traffic to take an unfamiliar exit. "Don't worry about it," he said.

"You and I are going to talk. That's all you need to know."

Gina swallowed a painful lump, terror clutching her chest. She needed an escape plan. Needed a clear head and a way to keep Tony calm. She had to buy the Winchesters some time to find her, if that would even be possible.

"What did you tell the police?" he demanded. "Whose truck were you in? That wasn't a woman's vehicle. Are you sleeping with that guy now? Going to tell him that's his baby you're carrying?"

Gina pressed her lips tight, refusing to voice the outrage building in her mind. Anger for his ridiculous misogyny. Fury for the implication she fell into bed with someone easily, as if she had time for any of that while running for her life. From him.

Tony swerved around slower-moving traffic, and a cacophony of blaring horns followed. "Well?" he demanded, slapping a hand down on her thigh and digging in with his fingers. "What did you tell the police? Did you cry them a river? Make yourself out to be a victim? Tell them I'm a bad guy?" He used a crybaby voice to ask the final question, then slammed his hand against the steering wheel a half-dozen times.

"You killed my apartment manager," she

snapped. "Attacked my friend and my doctor. Stabbed a deputy sheriff, attacked an innocent teenager and abducted my sister. You are a bad guy, Tony, and everyone is going to know it."

The crack of pain across her cheek sent lights dancing through her eyes.

He shook out his hand, as if the slap had hurt him, then flexed his fingers against the steering wheel. "You better not have told them any of those things. That woman was not your friend and that man wasn't your apartment manager. You don't even live there. You live with me!" He screamed the last word, while accelerating through a red light.

Gina's mind and body went numb. The throbbing of her cheek became part of a distant backdrop. She set her hands on her lap and erected the force field she needed to survive whatever was coming. It was time to disconnect. And think.

Lucas was working on a warrant for GPS tracking on the Marino company fleet, which included the SUV she was riding in. The family lawyers could only hold them off for so long, especially after he'd picked her up at the police station parking lot. Surely the department's security feed had captured that.

Meanwhile, she needed to stall Tony's plan, whatever that might be. She couldn't let him lock her up, constrain or injure her to a point that she couldn't run when the opportunity arose. That went for her sister as well.

She stole a glance in the rearview mirror, hoping Kayla showed signs of waking. Her little sister was thin and small, but Gina wasn't strong enough to carry her. Kayla had to wake up before Gina could run.

Slowly, the busier streets of an unfamiliar town bled into a residential neighborhood, thick with uninhabitable homes. Then an industrial park appeared up ahead.

Tony piloted the SUV through an open chain-link fence and into an area lined in warehouses and abandoned buildings.

She recognized the place after a long moment, though she'd never arrived by such a convoluted route. This was the location of his family's largest storage facility, where products for the stores were housed and shipped. It was also the place where Tony often held large, impromptu poker nights with friends, betting everything from stacks of cash to their high-end cars on a single hand.

He rolled the SUV to a stop outside a large bay door, then shifted into Park. "Do anything stupid, and I will shoot your sister," he said, then he climbed out and headed for the building.

Gina tracked him with her eyes and waited until his focus turned to the padlock. "Kayla!" she barked, twisting on her seat to smack her sister's knees. "Wake up! Kayla!"

Slowly, her sister's eyes opened, and a low moan rolled from her lips.

Gina's chest heaved with relief. "We're going to be okay, but you have to wake up."

Kayla tried to speak, the muffled sound barely permeating the silver tape across her lips. Her eyes were unfocused as she scanned the space, probably seeking Gina's face. Whatever Tony had given her was clearly still in control.

Gina faced front and stilled, unwilling to risk Tony seeing her turned around or talking. She covered her face with her hands and did her best to appear as if she was crying when he looked her way.

Outside, he shoved the warehouse door away, then headed back to the SUV.

"Tony's coming," Gina said quickly, behind the cover of her hand. "Pretend you're asleep. We have to make a plan."

The driver's door opened, and Tony climbed behind the wheel once more, then pulled smoothly into the warehouse. "Now, you and I are going to have that talk. You can start by explaining what kind of person would hide her pregnancy, then take a man's baby away from him." He jammed the shifter into Park and scowled. "What kind of mother are you going to be? Not a fit one, if you'd deny a child access to his father."

Gina scanned the scene beyond the windshield, mentally tallying her options for running or hiding.

"You lied to me, and you embarrassed me," he continued, irrationally outraged and betrayed. "You're going to have to apologize for that, and I'm not sure I can forgive you." He unfastened her seat belt, then jerked her across the console by her arm. "I want to see my baby."

Tony stared hard into her eyes before trailing his gaze down her body and lifting the hem of her shirt to stare at her gently rounded middle.

She gritted her teeth and turned her head away, fighting the weight of a thousand awful emotions.

He set a hot hand on her bare stomach, and she recoiled instinctively.

She tensed for another slap, but Tony shoved her off of him, then climbed out of the vehicle.

He circled the SUV while she scrambled back to her side, tugging her shirt into place. Then he opened the rear passenger door, and reached for her sister.

"Wait." Gina leaped out, eager to help Kayla, and ready to do anything she could to keep Tony's hands off of her. But it was too late.

He tossed Kayla over his shoulder like she was weightless and not even human, then began to move.

Gina rushed after them, down the massive aisles of metal shelving and boxed products meant for the outdoor outfitter stores. Eight-foot stuffed black bears stood beside racks of kayaks and pallets of ammunition. Tents, guns and hunting apparel filled every square inch of cavernous space. A thousand weapons he could use against her. Ten thousand ways he could do his worst.

Kayla's cheek bounced against Tony's back as he strode confidently through the rows of stock. Her eyes flashed open, and her gaze stuck to Gina.

Gina's heart sprinted with hope, and an idea came swiftly to mind. She fished the pepper spray Kayla had given her from her pocket, then passed it into her sister's hand.

"Don't touch her," Tony growled. He stopped and turned to catch Gina's wrist and pull her to his side. "She's off-limits to you. She's collateral."

They stopped at the end of the aisle, where a small living space had been arranged. A tent, a cot, a card table. Pop-up chairs and plastic coolers. He flipped Kayla off him, and she bounced onto the cot with a groan. Her limbs splayed, but there wasn't any sign of the pepper spray.

"Now," Tony said, spinning to face Gina, "I have to live like this because of you. Someone is staking out my house because of you. Watching my office and my folks' place. Because. Of. You. I can't go home. Can't do anything. And it's all your fault." He searched her face with angry eyes and gritted teeth, then his attention fell to her middle. "Show me my baby again."

Gina wet her lips and considered her options, which were few, then took the handful of steps to his side.

"That's right," he said. "Silent and obedient. Now lift your shirt."

Gina stopped short of his personal space, then slowly raised the hem of her shirt, exposing her midriff.

Behind him, red exit signs glowed over endless shelving. It wouldn't be easy, but she had to get there, and she had to take her sister with her.

Tony's hands snapped out and gripped her waist, then tugged her forward, until their bodies collided and his lips were mashed against hers.

She wrestled against him, and he did his best to keep her in place. Then her hand rose, on instinct, and she slapped his face.

The stillness between them lasted only a moment. Then his hand connected with her face once more.

She fell onto her hands and knees with sudden force and pain. A cry sprang from her lips, and infuriated tears began to fall. How was this happening? Again!

"Get up," he growled. "We're going inside the tent where you can apologize. Now!" He crouched over her, gripping her around the waist and attempting to haul her upright.

"No!" she yelled back, flailing and attempting to connect a foot or elbow somewhere that would count.

The burning scent of pepper spray rose around them, scorching her eyes, nose and throat. Tony yelled out as he released her and stumbled away, cursing violently from the pain.

Kayla grabbed Gina's elbow, and together, they ran.

Chapter Twenty-Three

Cruz had been inside the West Liberty Police Department for less than two minutes when he'd received the simple text.

911

Blaze had met him in the lobby with the to-go bags, bottles of water and a belated offer to help transfer their supplies from the Jeep to the truck.

How had there been enough time for something bad to happen?

Cruz and Blaze had made a run for the truck, until Cruz remembered he'd given the keys to Gina. Thankfully, Blaze had the Jeep keys, and the cousins were on the road inside a minute. But it hadn't mattered. The SUV and Gina were long gone.

Thankfully, Blaze had climbed behind the wheel, because Cruz was slowly losing his mind. Blaze's phone rang before they'd accessed the highway on-ramp, and he passed it to Cruz. "Answer," he said.

Lucas's name was on the screen.

"We're on the highway," Cruz said by way of greeting.

It was the only obvious choice for escape. Traffic was too heavy to get away downtown, and the SUV would be caught for sure on the quieter country roads. The highway, however, could take Tony and his victim anywhere in a matter of minutes.

"Good," Lucas said, his voice rising from the speaker. "We found a phone in the grass between the road and sidewalk. Looks like the one you gave her, Cruz. The photo on the lock screen is the view from your back deck."

Cruz grimaced and pressed one fist against his forehead, longing to chuck the phone out the window or otherwise burn off a burst of frustration any way he could. "What about the surveillance footage?"

"I'm going through that now," Lucas answered. "We've got her on camera leaving Blaze's truck and climbing into the SUV, but until it rolls forward, the vehicle is obstructed by the stone PD sign. It fits the make and model of the Marino company fleet, but I don't have a clear image of the driver or plate."

Blaze glanced at the phone as he navigated the busy highway. "Tell me we have enough to hurry the warrant along now, even without a clear image of the plate or driver."

"I'm working on it," Lucas said.

"Work faster," Cruz snapped. His grip tightened on the small, infuriating device. How much time did he have before Tony hurt her, or worse? Why would she have gone with him like that? He'd left her the keys. She could've driven away or honked the horn. Anything.

Then he realized. Tony had brought Kayla with him. He was sure of it.

Blaze changed lanes and increased his speed. "This is just like when Kayla was taken from her campus," he complained. "No proof Tony was behind the abduction. How can one guy be this slick?"

"I'm sure Kayla was with him in the SUV," Cruz said.

Understanding, then anger, crossed Blaze's features. "He used her as bait."

"He probably didn't even have to ask Gina to get in with him," Cruz said. "If Kayla was there, Gina wouldn't have hesitated."

Blaze activated his turn signal, then eased onto the next exit ramp. "That clears up why she got in," he said. "And how he convinced her to go so quickly. Now we just need an answer to where he took them."

"Hey," Lucas said. "Why don't you circle back, then we can press on the judge together. Get that warrant signed."

"On our way," Blaze said, already reentering the highway in the opposite direction.

"See ya then," Lucas said.

Cruz disconnected the call, his stomach sinking and aching impossibly more. It didn't matter that they hadn't had any specific direction as they'd cruised the highway. At least they'd been doing something, going somewhere. Turning back felt like a massive defeat.

The phone rang again as they merged with the flow of traffic. Derek's name appeared on the screen.

"Yeah," Cruz answered, activating the speaker option so Blaze could listen once more. "What do you have?"

"Me?" Derek asked, a hitch of confusion in his voice. "I thought you had something. I wanted in on it. Wait. Is this Cruz? Why are you on Blaze's phone?"

"I'm here," Blaze said. "We're in the Jeep, but I'm driving."

Silence stretched across the line.

"You're in the Jeep with Cruz," Derek repeated, finally speaking again. "Who's in your truck?"

"My truck's at the precinct," Blaze said. "No one is in it."

"No," Derek said. "Your truck is at the Marino company warehouse," he said. "I thought you'd found Gina and her sister. I'm headed there now, but I'm fifteen minutes out."

Blaze wrinkled his nose at the cell phone, then at Cruz before returning his eyes to the road. "We're in the Jeep. The truck's in the lot."

Cruz's heart leaped as sudden recognition hit. "She's got your keys," he said. "I gave them to her when I ran inside to grab the food. She's got your keys." He repeated the initial statement more slowly, a geyser of hope rising in his chest.

"I put a tracker on those," Derek said, the sound of his car's engine growing louder across the line. "Y'all better get out to the warehouse. And bring backup."

Gina choked and coughed as she stumbled, almost blindly, through the warehouse, pulled and guided by her sister.

Kayla's strides were awkward and sluggish, but she could see, and that was more than Gina could manage with the burn of pepper spray on her skin and in her lungs.

"I'm so sorry," Kayla whispered repeatedly as she towed Gina over the smooth concrete floor. "I couldn't get him without hitting you."

"It's okay." Gina's throat tightened on the words, and she began to cough again. She wanted to say more, to comfort and praise her sister, but her breaths were hard and shallow. The fire in her eyes, nose and throat was almost too much to handle.

Kayla pulled Gina in a new direction, then pressed her shoulder to a thick metal pole. "Here," she said, releasing her for the first time since they'd made their escape. "I found the foodstuff section. There's water."

Gina doubled over, rubbing her eyes and willing her lungs to collect more air.

Kayla's hand was on Gina's face a moment later. She pushed Gina's hands away and pried open her right eye. A thick splash of cold water hit her face.

Gina sucked air and blinked, trying not to make more noise than possible in response. Her nose ran and she longed to sob, but feared she'd give away their position. Tony was surely not far behind.

Kayla pressed a bottle into Gina's hand. "Use it. Hurry," she whispered, sounding utterly exhausted. "There's more if you need it, but we have to keep moving, and I'm not sure how long I can stay awake."

Gina followed her sister's instructions, splashing her left eye and wetting her hands to wash her face. Slowly, her vision returned with a blurry, patchy view. The nearest exit sign was a red smear above a door that was still a few aisles away. "Ready," she whispered, then turned to seek her sister.

Kayla leaned heavily against the shelving, her head supported by its metal frame.

"Come on," Gina whispered, wrapping her sister's arm around her shoulder, then willing herself to be strong. "You can't stop now," she said. "We're almost free. I know you can fight it a little longer."

Kayla leaned into Gina's assist with a groan.

A hellacious crash rooted her, temporarily, in place. Around them, the warehouse seemed to quake with the feral yell that followed. "Gina!" Tony's scream raised the hair on her arms and back of her neck to attention. Her heart caught in her already scorching throat, and she forced her feet forward, away from the sounds.

Kayla's head rolled against Gina's shoulder, and her legs twisted uselessly with each small step.

"No," Gina whispered, tugging Kayla's arm and nudging her with her hip. "Wake up."

Kayla moaned and her knees buckled.

Another enormous crash boomed and echoed through the building, like a thousand metal plates or capsizing grills.

Gina tipped slightly forward to accommodate her sister's weight, then began to race toward the exit.

A booming gunshot caused her steps to falter, but she didn't stop. Falling items to her left and right made her think Tony wasn't seeing much more clearly than she was just yet. And that might be what saved her life.

"Gina!" He followed her name with a long string of hate-filled words and vicious, gruesome threats. His heavy footfalls slapped the concrete floor behind her.

The next bullet whizzed past her head, colliding with a sack of feed that exploded and released its contents in a gush.

She gasped and felt the hot, slick tears roll over her stinging cheeks. She couldn't let her life end this way, in a warehouse begging for Tony's mercy. Couldn't be his victim one last time. And she absolutely would not allow her baby sister to die at the hands of her personal monster.

Fresh resolve rushed through her blood and

pumped her limbs. Kayla became lighter with the resurgence of will and determination.

Outside, the cry of police sirens launched a spout of hope in her powerful enough to do whatever it took for her to survive.

"Freeze!" a familiar voice bellowed as the sounds of emergency vehicles grew louder. "West Liberty PD," Blaze announced. "Anthony Marino, put the gun down and get your hands up where I can see them. You are under arrest."

Gina's chest heaved with relief as she reached, then pressed her shoulder against the exit door.

"Gina!" Cruz's voice reached her before he came into view. His arms wound around her and Kayla a moment later. "Medic!" he called over her head. "Here!"

"He drugged her," Gina croaked. "She won't wake up."

Cruz pulled Kayla into his arms. "What happened to your face?" he asked Gina, moving swiftly toward an arriving ambulance.

"Pepper spray."

EMTs exited the vehicle and took Kayla from Cruz's arms.

He turned to Gina immediately and pressed her to his chest. "Did he do anything else to you? To your baby?"

Gina sobbed at the memory of Tony's hand on her stomach, of his palm connecting with her face. "I think we're okay," she said, her limbs beginning to tremble. "How'd you find us?"

"Derek tracks us, and you have Blaze's keys," he said, his lips tipping into a small smile. "Also, your friend Celia called the phone you left with Lucas. She said she told her boyfriend about your exchange, and he told Tony. She didn't expect that to happen," he said. "She called as soon as she could, but we were already on our way."

"Hey." An approaching paramedic raised one hand in greeting. "Did I hear you say pepper spray?"

She squinted against the bright midday light and nodded, her face still on fire.

"Gina," Cruz said. "This is my cousin Isaac. Why don't we ride with him to the hospital. Kayla will be there, and you can make your rounds to visit Dr. Tulane and Heather. We can call your folks on the way."

A bubble of hope rose in Gina's chest as she let the men help her into the ambulance. "Heather and Dr. Tulane are awake?"

He nodded. "We can stop by and bug Rex and Deputy Stone while we're at it."

"Yes," she said. "Please. I have so much to say to all of them."

Isaac pointed to the gurney. "Then why don't you have a seat, and we'll get you checked out."

She agreed easily, then watched as Kayla's ride wound to life and zoomed away.

"She's going to be okay," Cruz said. "So are you."

A few minutes passed as Isaac examined her briefly and flushed her eyes. When he moved away, she watched through open ambulance bay doors as Blaze stuffed Tony into a police cruiser, then patted the roof with one hand. Knox smiled brightly as he piloted the car away from the warehouse.

"You okay?" Cruz asked, pressing a kiss to the side of her head and squeezing her hand in his.

"I am now," she said, moving her attention away from the cruiser and fixing it on the man beside her. "Thank you for being my hero," she whispered, tugging him down to meet her lips.

"Always."

Chapter Twenty-Four

Gina sighed at the familiar sight of Derek and Allison's house along the river. Spring had come to Kentucky in an explosion of color, and the truth of that could be seen all around their property. The Winchesters were having their weekly dinner, and Gina couldn't wait to see them all again. Cruz had even bought her a new dress, two sizes larger than her pre-pregnancy clothes, thanks to the baby weight she was still carrying, two months after giving birth. The dress was white eyelet, and he claimed to love the way it looked against her olive skin. She suspected the way it danced around her thighs didn't hurt, but whatever kept his eyes on her was perfect. Not that she'd ever had any trouble holding his attention, even when she'd nearly outgrown her maternity clothes a few months ago. Cruz always thought she looked beautiful, and he told her so often, she even believed it.

A major sign of emotional healing, according to her therapist.

Cruz, on the other hand, had worn a simple black V-neck T-shirt with his usual nicely fitting jeans. He looked like a romance novel cover model.

Gina took a moment to admire the acres of bluegrass, the tidy flower beds and the abundance of baby animals in pens and pastures before climbing out of the Jeep. She had a new appreciation for the mamas with their offspring since she'd joined their ranks in February, with the help of a fully recovered Dr. Tulane. Her daughter, Angelique Marie Ricci, had been born three weeks early, but she was absolutely perfect, and Gina could barely remember life without her.

Cruz unfastened his seat belt and grinned. "Looks like the gang's all here," he said.

"Aren't they always?" she asked, climbing carefully down from the Jeep.

Derek had the most land and interior square footage of all the Winchesters, not to mention animals and an adorable toddler to draw the family to his place every Sunday. This night was no exception. Though there seemed to be more cars than usual.

"Is that my parents' car?" Gina asked.

Cruz pulled the baby carrier from the back

seat, then met Gina on the grass with Angelique. "Looks like." He kissed Gina gently before taking her hand and leading her toward the rear deck, where sounds of music, chatter and laughter rose into the twilight. "You sure you don't mind spending another night over here, surrounded by all these Winchesters?" he asked. "We're here every weekend, and I know you're tired. It'd be fine if you'd rather have a nap."

Gina smiled. "I am tired, but you get up at night with Angelique just as often as I do," she said. "And I like seeing your family. They always have such great stories. And food." She linked her arm with his, enjoying the moment and warm evening breeze. "And apparently I get to see my folks too."

Cruz's family had become an extension of her own last fall, and she'd moved into his house permanently only a few months after Tony had gone to jail. Her relationship with Cruz had grown exponentially and at breakneck speed from there. Moving in with him so soon after what she'd been through with Tony probably seemed like a mistake to some folks, but she'd never doubted her decision. In fact, she still thought about pinching herself most mornings, just to be sure she wasn't dreaming. The only thing she adored as much as her daughter and Cruz was his crazy family and the way they got along with hers. A massive holiday party at her parents' home had confirmed what Cruz had suggested shortly after he'd met Gina. The Winchesters and Riccis made fast friends. They'd mingled for hours, and lasting friendships were forged over tiramisu and eggnog.

She and Cruz turned at the sound of an incoming vehicle, then waited while Lucas and his wife, Gwen, climbed down from their truck.

Gwen met Gina with a hug. "Sorry we're late."

"I'm just glad you're here," Gina said.

Gwen had become like a sister to Gina during the winter, when the pair had bonded over their past traumas and present love of Winchester men. Nowadays, Gina looked forward to seeing her at each family gathering and catching up on anything she'd missed.

Lucas loosened his tie and unbuttoned his dress shirt at the collar. "The judge denied the Marino family's appeals," he said, a small smile blooming on his newly shaven face. "I thought she would, but I went anyway, just in case anyone needed a reminder on the severity of Tony's crimes. They didn't. Judge Hawthorne made it clear Tony will stay behind bars for a very long time. Probably the rest of his life, without parole."

Gina crossed the bit of space between them and hugged Lucas, catching him off guard as usual.

Gwen laughed.

"She's a hugger," Cruz said, the smile evident in his voice.

Lucas patted Gina's back. "We've all got you," he said. "You don't have to worry about anything anymore."

She stepped away with a smile. "I know." She'd spent the past six months in therapy, working through all the issues Tony had caused her, and thanks to all her outside support, she felt stronger every week. "Thank you."

A sharp whistle drew the group's attention to the rear of the home, where Lucas's mom, Cruz's aunt, waved a hand overhead. "Are y'all coming over here? Or do we need to come over there?"

Gwen laughed, then led Lucas in his mama's direction. He swiped the baby carrier from Cruz's hand on his way past. "We've got Angelique," he said. "You two lovebirds take your time."

Gina snuggled against Cruz's side as they walked, reveling in her good fortune and gratitude. She'd been through the unthinkable, but she'd gained a fairy tale, and she wouldn't change it for anything in the world.

An array of bistro lights came into view, strung randomly through the trees and above and around the deck. Several tables had been lined along the perimeter. One of those was packed with food, the rest with people. Winchesters, Riccis and a smattering of cops, detectives and friends.

"What's going on?" Gina asked Cruz softly as the little crowd quieted and smiled at their arrival.

"Baby!" Gina's mom cooed. "Come here." She pulled Gina into a hug, then passed her to her father and sister.

Gina laughed. "I didn't know you guys were coming," she said. "It's so good to see you."

"Well, we weren't about to miss this," Kayla said, looking as if Gina had grown a second head.

Gina smiled, thankful every day for the full recovery her little sister had made from her overdose at Tony's hand. She, too, was still in counseling for the trauma, and Gina enjoyed the occasional session they shared together.

She'd thought her family was close before, but the horrors they'd endured only served to strengthen their already tight bonds.

"Miss what?" she asked, frowning at Kayla's bright smile.

The volume on the stereo lowered, and the song changed to a ballad Cruz had deemed their song on New Year's Eve. That same song had been playing the night he'd first told her he loved her, and on the night she'd officially moved in.

"Cruz?"

She turned to seek his face for an explanation, but he wasn't at her side any longer.

Instead, he knelt on the ground, a small velvet box in his hand. Cruz pinched the lid between his thumb and first finger, then raised it to reveal a simple diamond solitaire. "This was my mama's," Cruz said, his voice cracking slightly on the words. He cleared his throat, then raised the box to her in one hand, wearing his trademark grin. He reached for her fingers with his free hand, then curled them gently in his. "Gina Marie Ricci."

She gasped, and the ragged, emotion-filled breath caused a round of chuckles and giggling from the crowd.

"I know we haven't been together long," Cruz said, "but I've been falling in love with you since the moment we met. I can't imagine living a life without you and Angelique in it.

And I'm hoping you'll do me the honor of letting me be your husband."

Gina nodded and laughed as tears pricked, then fell from her eyes.

He stood to wipe the drops from her cheeks. "Marry me?" he asked softly.

And Gina said, "Yes."

* * * * *

Don't miss the next books in Julie Anne Lindsey's Heartland Heroes miniseries, coming soon. And if you missed the previous books in the series, look for:

SVU Surveillance
Protecting His Witness
Kentucky Crime Ring

You'll find them wherever Harlequin Intrigue books are sold!

Get 4 FREE REWARDS!

We'll send you 2 FREE Books plus 2 FREE Mystery Gifts.

Harlequin Romantic Suspense books are heart-racing page-turners with unexpected plot twists and irresistible chemistry that will keep you guessing to the very end.

FREE
Value Over
$20

Get 4 FREE REWARDS!

We'll send you 2 FREE Books plus 2 FREE Mystery Gifts.

Harlequin Presents books feature the glamorous lives of royals and billionaires in a world of exotic locations, where passion knows no bounds.

FREE Value Over $20

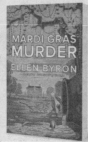 

HARLEQUIN SELECTS COLLECTION

19 FREE BOOKS IN ALL!

From Robyn Carr to RaeAnne Thayne to Linda Lael Miller and Sherryl Woods we promise (actually, GUARANTEE!) each author in the Harlequin Selects collection has seen their name on the *New York Times* or *USA TODAY* bestseller lists!

#2037 TARGETING THE DEPUTY
Mercy Ridge Lawmen • by Delores Fossen

After narrowly escaping an attempt on his life, Deputy Leo Logan is shocked to learn the reason for the attack is his custody battle for his son with his ex, Olivia Nash. To catch the real killer, he'll have to keep them both close—and risk falling for Olivia all over again.

#2038 CONARD COUNTY: CHRISTMAS BODYGUARD
Conard County: The Next Generation • by Rachel Lee

Security expert Hale Scribner doesn't get personal with clients. Ever. But having evidence that could put away a notoriously shady CEO doesn't make Allie Burton his standard low-risk charge. With an assassin trailing them 24/7, they'll need a Christmas miracle to survive the danger...and their undeniable attraction.

#2039 TEXAS ABDUCTION
An O'Connor Family Mystery • by Barb Han

When Cheyenne O'Connor's friend goes missing, she partners with her estranged husband, rancher Riggs O'Connor, for answers. During their investigation, evidence emerges suggesting their daughter—who everyone claims died at childbirth—might be alive and somehow connected. Riggs and Cheyenne are determined to find out what really happened...and if their little girl will be coming home after all.

#2040 MOUNTAINSIDE MURDER
A North Star Novel Series • by Nicole Helm

North Star undercover operative Sabrina Killian is on a hit man's trail and doesn't want help from Wyoming search and rescue ranger Connor Lindstrom. But the persistent ex-SEAL is the killer's real target. Will Sabrina and Connor's most dangerous secrets even the odds—or take them out for good?

#2041 ALASKAN CHRISTMAS ESCAPE
Fugitive Heroes: Topaz Unit • by Juno Rushdan

With an elite CIA kill squad locating hacker Zenobia Hanley's Alaska wilderness hideout, it's up to her mysterious SEAL neighbor, John Lowry, to save her from capture. Regardless of the risks and secrets they're both hiding, John's determined to protect Zee because there's more at stake this Christmas than just their lives...

#2042 BAYOU CHRISTMAS DISAPPEARANCE
by Denise N. Wheatley

Mona Avery is determined to investigate a high-profile missing person case in the Louisiana bayou before heading home for Christmas. Stubborn detective Dillon Reed insists she's more of a hindrance than a help. But when a killer wants Mona's story silenced, only Dillon can keep her safe...

YOU CAN FIND MORE INFORMATION ON UPCOMING HARLEQUIN TITLES,
FREE EXCERPTS AND MORE AT HARLEQUIN.COM.